RONALD ROLHEISER

Ronald Rolheiser OMI was born in Macklin, Saskatchewan, Canada. One of a large family, he was educated locally and after high school joined a missionary order. Eight years later, he completed a Masters degree in theology at the University of San Francisco, and then became a lecturer at Newman Theological College, Edmonton, Alberta. After teaching for six years, he went to the University of Louvain, Belgium, where he completed his doctorate.

In 1983, he rejoined the staff at Newman College as a professor of systematic theology and spirituality, and as Vice-Dean of theology. He has also taught in Fort Wright College, Washington; The American College, Louvain, Belgium; All Hallows College, Dublin; and at Seattle University, Washington. Besides teaching he leads retreats and enjoys sport, both as a participant and a spectator. He writes a regular column for several newspapers, including the *Catholic Herald*.

Of *The Restless Heart*, consultant psychiatrist Dr Jack Dominian has written: 'Loneliness is a characteristic all of us experience. It can be destructive when we feel alienated from God, fellow human beings, work and nature. It can be enriching when it becomes the basis for the thirst for God, beauty, knowledge and truth, for love and union with others, emotionally and sexually. Father Rolheiser covers admirably the roots of the restlessness of human loneliness and provides, probably for the first time, an eminently readable Christian response to it. This is not a book to read for an answer to all the problems of loneliness, but for the ability of the author to move us from the danger of the condition to its immense opportunities.'

Ronald Rolheiser

THE RESTLESS HEART

First printed in Great Britain 1988
First published by Dimension Books, Inc., Denville,
New Jersey, USA

Spire is an imprint of Hodder and Stoughton Limited

British Library Cataloguing in Publication Data

Rolheiser, Ronald
The restless heart.
1. Loneliness – Christian viewpoints
I. Title
248.4

ISBN 0-340-49046-2

*Printed in Great Britain for Hodder and Stoughton Limited, Mill Road, Dunton
Green, Sevenoaks, Kent by Richard Clay Limited, Bungay, Suffolk. Photoset by
Rowland Phototypesetting Limited, Bury St Edmunds, Suffolk.*

Hodder and Stoughton Editorial Office: 47 Bedford Square, London WC1B 3DP.

CONTENTS

ACKNOWLEDGMENTS

The author wishes to thank the following for permission to quote material from these publications.

Excerpt from Carl R. Rogers, *On Becoming a Person*, copyright © 1961 by Carl R. Rogers. Used by permission of Houghton Mifflin Company.

Excerpts from *The Collected Works of St. John of the Cross*, translated by Kieran Kavanaugh and Otilio Rodriguez, copyright © 1964 by Washington Province of Discalced Carmelites, Inc. Paperback edition published by ICS Publications, 2131 Lincoln Road, N.E. Washington, D.C. 20002 USA.

Excerpts from *Poustinia* by Catherine de Hueck Doherty, copyright 1975, Ave Maria Press, Notre Dame, Ind., reprinted with permission of the publisher.

Excerpts from the Revised Standard Version of the Bible, copyrighted 1946, 1952, © 1971, 1973.

Excerpts from *The Stone Angel*, by Margaret Laurence, reprinted by permission of The Canadian Publishers, McClelland and Stewart Limited, Toronto.

Excerpt from Alvin Toffler, *Future Shock*, copyright 1970, Random House Inc., New York, N.Y.

Excerpt from Albert Camus, *The Fall*, translated by Justin O'Brien, copyright 1963, Alfred A. Knopf, Inc., New York, N.Y.

Excerpt from John Steinbeck, *The Grapes of Wrath*, Viking Penguin Inc., New York, N.Y., copyright 1966.

Excerpt from *Studies in the Psychology of Mystics*, Joseph Marechal, Magi Books Inc., Albany, N.Y., copyright 1964.

Excerpt from *From Glory to Glory*, Gregory of Nyssa,

translated by Jean Danielou and H. Musurillo, published by Charles Scribner's Sons, New York, N.Y., copyright 1961.

Excerpt from *Listen to Pain with Heart* by Henri Nouwen, in *National Catholic Reporter*, Sept. 6, 1974. Reprinted by permission of the *National Catholic Reporter*, P.O. Box 281, Kansas City, Mo. 64141.

Excerpt from *Gate of Heaven* by Ralph McInerney, Harper and Row, San Francisco, copyright 1975.

Excerpt from *The Hills Beyond* 'God's Lonely Man' by Thomas Wolfe, Signet Classic, New York, copyright 1968.

Excerpts from the Jerusalem Bible. Copyrighted 1966, 1967, 1968. Doubleday & Company, Inc., Garden City, New York.

FOREWORD

Without a doubt Father Rolheiser is the most communicative theologian I have yet come across. His writing and his lectures have been of enormous help to me personally, and I feel that this book, which explains the deep spiritual significance of human loneliness and longing, will become a classic.

Delia Smith
June 1988

PREFACE

On February 12, 1944, thirteen-year-old Anne Frank wrote the following words in her now-famous diary:

> Today the sun is shining, the sky is a deep blue, there is a lovely breeze and I am longing – so longing for everything. To talk, for freedom, for friends, to be alone.
>
> And I do so long . . . to cry! I feel as if I am going to burst, and I know that it would get better with crying; but I can't, I'm restless, I go from room to room, breathe through the crack of a closed window, feel my heart beating, as if it is saying, 'can't you satisfy my longing at last?'
>
> I believe that it is spring within me, I feel that spring is awakening, I feel it in my whole body and soul. It is an effort to behave normally. I feel utterly confused. I don't know what to read, what to write, what to do, I only know that I am longing.

There is in all of us, at the very centre of our lives, a tension, an aching, a burning in the heart that is insatiable, non-quietable and very deep. Sometimes, we experience this longing as focused on a person, particularly if we are in a love that is not consummated. Other times we experience this yearning as a longing to attain something.

Most often, though, it is a longing without a clear name or focus, an aching that cannot be clearly pinpointed or described. Like Anne Frank, we only know that we are restless, full of disquiet, aching at a level that we cannot seem to get at.

Why is it so difficult for us to be restful and satisfied? What is it within the human spirit that makes us so incurably erotic, full of wanderlust and nostalgia?

Shakespeare talked of 'immortal longings', Karl Rahner, the German theologian, speaks about the 'torment of the insufficiency of everything attainable.'

This book will look at these questions from both a humanistic and a religious point of view. It will attempt, in a way that does not pretend to be definitive, to give some answers, to show that this fundamental dis-ease within human beings can be healthy, that it comes from the way God made us. It will also show that it can be very dangerous.

Because our hearts are so incurably restless, we go through life filled both with the potential for greatness and for destruction. Restlessness pushes us relentlessly outward. In some senses, it is our soul.

St Augustine once prayed: 'You have made us for yourself, Lord, and our hearts are restless until they rest in you!' This book will attempt to explain what is implied in that.

I would, before closing this Preface, like to express my gratitude to all who helped bring this book together: my religious community, my family, the Trappist community of Lafayette, Oregon, and especially the students at Newman Theological College, Edmonton, Alberta, who discussed these ideas with me. I owe a debt of thanks too to Delia Smith, Charlotte Beler, Sharon Harry, and the editors at Hodder and Stoughton for the editorial work.

The book is entitled, THE RESTLESS HEART. Commenting on restlessness, Karl Rahner once remarked that, in this life, 'all symphonies remain unfinished.' It is for those who struggle with restlessness and the unfinished symphony that this book is written.

Ronald Rolheiser
Newman Theological College
April 16, 1988

PART I:
THE NATURE OF LONELINESS

1

THE PROBLEM

The grip of loneliness

No person has ever walked our earth and been free from the pains of loneliness. Rich and poor, wise and ignorant, faith-filled and agnostic, healthy and unhealthy, have all alike had to face and struggle with its potentially paralysing grip. It has granted no immunities. To be human is to be lonely.

To be human, however, is also to respond. The human person has always responded to this pain. The response has varied greatly. Sometimes loneliness has led us to new heights of creativity, and sometimes it has led us to drugs, alcohol, and emotional paralysis; sometimes it has led us to the true encounter of love and authentic sexuality, sometimes it has led us into dehumanising relationships and destructive sexuality; sometimes it has moved us to greater depth of openness towards God and others, to fuller life, and sometimes it has led us to jump off bridges, to end life; sometimes it has given us a glimpse of heaven, sometimes it has given us a glimpse of hell; sometimes it has made the human spirit, sometimes it has broken it; always it has affected it. For loneliness is one of the deepest, most universal, and most profound experiences that we have.

Even if you are a relatively happy person, a person who

relates easily to others and who has many close friends, you are probably still lonely at times. If you are a very sensitive person, the type who feels things deeply, you are probably, to some degree, lonely all the time.

However, most of us appear reluctant to admit our loneliness, even to ourselves. All of us seem to have a congenital need to deny that we experience loneliness and that it is, in some way, responsible for many of our feelings, actions and pursuits. We try to distance ourselves from it, not admitting to ourselves and to others that we are lonely. We admit that we are lonely only with a feeling of shame and weakness. As well, most of us feel that loneliness is not something that should affect normal, healthy persons. We identify it much more with those that our society considers marginal persons, namely, the elderly, the unwanted, the unlovable, the alienated, and those others who for one reason or another seem divorced from the mainstream of life. We never imagine for a moment that we should be subject to intense feelings of loneliness.

Under the surface, though, we are not easily fooled by our own façade of strength. We hurt, and we live in pain, in loneliness, damned loneliness. Unfortunately, too, the cost of our self-deception is high. We pay a heavy price for not admitting our loneliness, facing it squarely, and grappling with it honestly. Loneliness, as we shall see, is most dangerous when it is not recognised, accepted, and worked through creatively. It is then that it wreaks havoc with our lives. Conversely, too, we shall see that it is a tremendously creative and humanising force when it is recognised and lived correctly.

The hidden face of loneliness

Despite our denials of loneliness, evidence for it is everywhere. It does not require professional insight, nor much documentation, to affirm the fact that as a society, and as individuals, we are lonely. All one needs to do is to look around oneself, or deeply inside oneself, to see evidence of loneliness, staggering, painful evidence. For example, even a quick look at the grim statistics which document the use of alcohol, drugs (both hard and soft), the sale of pornographic materials, and the number of suicides, tells us that we are a lonely people, living in pain.[1] In our Western world, we consume millions of pounds of tranquillisers and barbiturates annually. At the same time each year we see an incrēase in the number of persons who are seeking professional counselling, suffering from nervous strain and mental disorders, getting involved in encounter groups, sensitivity groups, religious fads, newer forms of communal and marital living, and in promiscuous sexuality.

Granted, all these things are not necessarily indicative of loneliness; other factors are often present. However, loneliness is certainly a large factor in bringing many of these phenomena about.

We see concomitant phenomena in other areas. Over recent decades, we have seen the motif of loneliness emerging more and more within philosophy, art, literature, psychology, and within religious and social thought. The so-called pop arts, modern music, movies, literature, popular magazines, and the like, have also focused much on loneliness as one of their major and more interesting themes.[2] The prevalence and popularity of this theme in so much recent thought and art suggests that our human hearts tend to resonate when we hear talk of loneliness.

Perhaps the clearest example of this is popular music. Music, like other art forms, becomes popular only when it communicates some human experience. The popularity, therefore, of much of our modern rock music, particularly of the poorer variety, is confusing to people who judge music solely by the quality of its melody, harmony, symmetry, and lyrics. Much of our modern rock music, in comparison to classical music, is weak in all these aspects. Yet millions flock to listen to this music, to buy recordings of it. Why? The reason is quite simply that it speaks to people. In some ways, and at various times in our lives, these grinding guitars and booming drums (complete with a writhing singer) capture more explicitly the confusion, the torment, the pain, and the loneliness of our minds than do the symphonies of Beethoven and other such classics. In many ways, the rock music of our age speaks to our culture in the way the 'blues' spoke to the oppressed and enslaved blacks during their days of enslavement. We like a music when 'it fits,' when it strikes a chord inside us!

Who more acutely symbolises the pain of our age than the gyrating, writhing rock singer, screaming into an ultra-sensitive microphone, nearly drowned out by guitars and drums, trying desperately to communicate, to penetrate someone's ears and heart – if in no other way, than at least through the sheer force of sound? His records sell because the gyrating and writhing of his music and his body is not unlike our minds and hearts which also gyrate and writhe as they struggle to communicate, struggle to make contact, struggle to penetrate, struggle to pierce the riddle which separates us from the minds and hearts of others. We, too, are desperately trying to communicate, in whatever fashion possible!

However, even if there were no poets, no artists, no musicians, no professional commentators to point out our loneliness to us, we would still be acutely aware of being lonely; the voice of our heart, most often making itself heard through pain, is more than sufficient to tell us this.

We are many different persons who make up the human race. Regardless of our differences, and regardless of whatever hand of cards life has dealt us, our hearts all speak the same language, the language of love. Part of the language of love, though, is also the language of pain and loneliness. We yearn for full, all-consuming love, and ecstatic union with God or with others. Reality, however, does not always deal in dreams and yearnings. Consequently, we go through life experiencing not just love, but frustration, restlessness, tension, and loneliness as well. In life, all of us are somewhat frustrated in our deep desire to share our being and our richness with others. We live knowing that others do not fully know and understand us, and that others can never fully know and understand us, that they are 'out there' and we are 'in here'. St Paul calls this, living as 'through a glass, darkly', a riddle, a veil, a mist of unreality which separates us from God and others, and from what is authentically real (1 Cor. 13:12–13).

Our hearts were not built to live as through a 'glass, darkly', but to be in consummate union with God and others. And so, as we try to sort our way through the mist of unreality, the riddle of life, our hearts are lonely and, thus, speak to us of not just love, but also of pain. At times the pain is not so poignant and we feel close to God and others. At other times, the pain becomes unbearable and we are given a foretaste of hell, realising that loneliness is the ultimate threat, the final terror which can relativise all else. Mostly, though, the pain is tolerable, but nagging: a dissatisfaction with the quality of our life and our relationships to people, a frustration without an object, a yearning without a particular reference, a nostalgia for past moments and friends, a restlessness which prevents us from relaxing and from being present to the moment, a feeling of alienation, a paranoia, a sense of missing out on something, an inexplicable emptiness.

Too often, though, we run from these feelings of loneliness, thinking that there is something wrong with us. We guard our loneliness from others, keeping it private, like an object of shame. Yet other hearts speak the same language as ours. Carl Rogers once said:

I have almost invariably found that the very feeling which has seemed to me most private, most personal and hence, most incomprehensible by others, has turned out to be an expression for which there is a resonance in many people. It has led me to believe that what is most personal and unique in each of us is probably the very element which would, if it were shared and expressed, speak most deeply to others.[3]

Our experience of loneliness is surely such an experience; perhaps the very one that Rogers had most in mind. Loneliness is not a rare and curious phenomenon. It is at the centre of every person's ordinary life experience. The pain of loneliness is the pain of unconsummated love. We do a lot of daydreaming about fulfilment and, on days when the pain gets bad, perhaps we cry a little. But mostly we are silent, silent about our loneliness and the deep pulses inside us which make our being tick.

An intensifying problem

The problem of loneliness, obviously, is not a new problem, unique to our age. Human beings have always been lonely. However, it is the belief of many that we are in our Western world experiencing loneliness with a much greater intensity than ever before. Why? I suggest several interconnected reasons:

First of all, because of the amount of leisure time which our culture affords us, we have the luxury of being able to focus on our more interpersonal needs. Up until recent generations people simply had less time and energy to spare for their emotional and spiritual needs. Most of their time and energy had, of necessity, to be spent at long hours of work, often physical and tiring. For example, many of our parents and grandparents spent much of their time and energies simply surviving, responding to the harsh dictates of their situation in history, coping with the economic depression, struggling as immigrants to be accepted, to learn a new language, to find a decent job, to build and pay for a home, and to educate their family. They laboured, often inhumanly, to move themselves from 'rags to riches', economically and socially. This consumed most of their time, energy, and creativity.

Today, mainly because of their work, the whole situation is drastically changed. We, their offspring, are born into the affluence and privilege that they worked so hard to create. We no longer need to spend huge chunks of time, energy, and creativity on many of the issues which absorbed them. As a result, given affluence and leisure time, we almost automatically focus more on our emotional and spiritual needs – or we spend a lot of time and money trying to distract ourselves from having to focus on them. We have the luxury, perhaps never before afforded a people, of being able to experience our loneliness in its utmost depth. Leisure time and affluence, because they have taken away from us the need to struggle to survive physically, have helped to throw us back upon ourselves and forced us to search for deeper meaning, interpersonal and spiritual. It has produced, as some would call it, a 'higher psychological temperature'. This has allowed for a certain liberation of psychological and spiritual energy, at least potentially so. However, the energy released by affluence and leisure is generally inchoate, not clearly focused, and usually not even explicitly recognised as a positive energy. It is experienced more as a restlessness, a driving force pushing us into things, a loneliness.

It is no accident, therefore, that we spend billions on entertainment, on alcohol, on travel, and on just about anything which promises to give us some respite from the restlessness inside of us.

Adding to the buildup of intensity is the fact, well analysed by sociologists, of the fragmentation of our society. The nineteenth-century sociologist, Ferdinand Tonnies, has analysed this most succinctly with his famous distinction between a *Gemeinschaft* and a *Gesellschaft* society. Formerly, we lived in what was largely a *Gemeinschaft* society, a society characterised by the extended family, where anonymity and privacy were rare, and there was little mobility, geographical or social. Today, we are for the most part in a *Gesellschaft* society, one characterised by the nuclear family, anonymity, and much mobility. This switch, while it has in many ways provided us with greater freedom to relate to others as we choose, has at the same time, paradoxically, helped generate and intensify loneliness by undercutting much of the interdependence which was foundational for many of our previous relationships. As we become more of a *Gesellschaft* society, we seek our privacy and freedom with a passion, not wanting any interdependence forced upon us. We want to be free to choose the persons with whom we will relate, and the depth to which we will relate. So, at marriage, we break away from our own family to try to create our own private, nuclear family. We seek our own private life, with a private house, a private car, a private office, and, not content with that, we want within our home, a private room, a private telephone, a private television, and so on. And, once we have attained that, and systematically undercut many of our interdependencies with other people, then we wonder why we are lonely. We live in huge cities, among millions of people, and we relate, in a meaningful way, to very few; partly because in so many areas of our lives there is no longer any need to share with others. We seek our privacy and freedom with a righteous zeal, and often intensify our own loneliness as we attain them.

Our feelings of loneliness are intensified still further by what is known as 'Future Shock', which has been analysed most astutely by Alvin Toffler. Although Toffler does not apply his thesis very directly to the problem of loneliness, he well might. According to Toffler, as the future breaks into the present, we experience that *people, places, objects, organisations*, and *knowledge* pass through our lives in an ever more rapid way. Formerly, it was not uncommon to relate to the same set of people (family and friends), the same geographical locale (usually the place of our birth), the same organisations (Church and social clubs) and to the same knowledge (what we had learned in school and college generally remained true) for much of, or perhaps for even all of, our lives. Now with the pace of life ever increasing in tempo, with technology and knowledge literally exploding around us, and with constant mobility, we find that we relate to few things, and often few persons, for very long. They are here today, and gone tomorrow! The result is often an increase in loneliness.

Toffler aptly compares this with what happens in the phenomenon of 'Cultural Shock'. For instance, if someone were to pick us up and suddenly transport us into a totally new land, among new people, with a new language, a different ethic, and a whole way of life radically different from our own, we would suffer 'Cultural Shock', part of the pain of which would be an intense feeling of loneliness, of being cut off from our roots. 'Future Shock' is dynamically the same. As more and more people pass through our lives, and as we move from place to place, pulling up our roots, jettisoning houses, cars, organisational memberships (and not infrequently marriage partners and human relationships as well), it is not surprising that we are growing more lonely.

Finally, coupled with all of this is the influence of modern media, especially advertising, which fan the flames of our loneliness, often bringing it to a volcanic peak. Our television sets, our magazines, our cinemas, and much of our advertising present many of our ideals of love and intimacy, of freedom and community, of laughter and presence, as having already been attained – by others! Constantly on our screens and in our magazines, we see persons who have already seemingly broken through the riddle of loneliness and have already attained the things that our heart wants but can never seem to attain. And so we spend hours watching and envying these people who are presented to us as having already attained redemption. We watch and envy their exciting lives, their zest, their humour, their intimacy with each other, and of course, their tanned beautiful bodies, their freedom, and their never-ending supply of money! Seeing other people attain love and intimacy, even if just on a screen, cannot help but fan the flames of our own torrid hearts. Our own lives, fraught with pettiness and eczema which also make up part of reality, never seem to measure up to those lives we see on our movie and television screens. We live as through 'a glass, darkly'; they do not. Thus our own feelings of frustration, inadequacy, and loneliness intensify.

I remember as a young teenager watching the Pepsi, Coke, and 7-Up ads on television. The young people doing them were always handsome, beautiful people, tanned and smiling, celebrating life with gusto and zest, running with their faces to the wind, in soft green forests, hand in hand, embracing without hesitation, obviously at ease with themselves, each other, and life. An advertisement like that was always, for me, a mirror; a painful mirror which helped me to see myself, pimpled and unfree, lacking gusto, zest, and a sense of celebration, hesitant and halting in relationships, usually without someone with whom to walk hand in hand, ill-at-ease, but searching, a lonely teenager, spending more than a few hours shuffling hesitantly in the stag line, with a deep feeling of loneliness and inadequacy burning away inside me.

Modern media and advertising, far too often, have left us with the feeling that the riddle of loneliness can be pierced; others have done it, and are not so lonely as we are. We are among the few who are missing out on life. This has played more than a minor role in intensifying the loneliness within us.

Human beings have always been lonely. Loneliness, as we will see later, stems from our very structure as a human being. However, our loneliness today seems to be intensifying, swelling, stepping up its tempo and slowly building into a crescendo which threatens to break at some future date.

2

THE DANGERS OF LONELINESS

Loneliness: danger and opportunity

Loneliness can be for us a great opportunity for growth. However, like most worthwhile things, it comes to us fraught with danger. Few forces can wreak as much havoc with our lives as can loneliness. Its force, if not recognised and handled in a meaningful and creative way, can be extremely dangerous. It can, with alternating pulses, paralyse our energies or propel us into destructive activity. Why? What are these dangers?

Here I would like to isolate and speak briefly about *six* potential dangers stemming from our loneliness:

The hidden cost: the dangers of loneliness

(1) *Loneliness, if not understood, can be destructive of human intimacy and love*

Loneliness can, and often does, effectively damage our relationships. Usually it is not recognised as playing much of a role in our ordinary day-to-day relationships; yet, under the surface, it is most frequently the canker which causes so much of our search for love and intimacy to be frustrating. A few examples will help to illustrate this:

Loneliness can lead to over-possessiveness in relationships

Because we are lonely, we very often become jealous and overly possessive of our friends and loved ones. We need love so badly that, often when we do find it, we try to seize it too strongly. We become 'clammy and sticky', making unfair impositions on the freedom of the loved one. Because our loneliness makes us so desperate for intimacy, we are often unable to allow our friends and loved ones space to be themselves, to come and go freely, and to have room to grow according to their own inner dictates. Rather our own lonely needs frequently cause us to choke relationships to death, with jealousy, with unfair demands for time, for affection, for exclusiveness.

Instead of rejoicing when our friends succeed at things, or when they find other friendships which are supportive for them, we become jealous and fearful lest we might lose their friendship. We demand exclusiveness and try to possess our loved ones as we would a prized object. This, perhaps more than anything else, is harmful to friendship and intimacy. From our own experience, we know that few things sour a relationship and alienate us as quickly from others as does jealousy and over-possessiveness. As soon as we sense this developing within a relationship we usually run, from the unfair bondage, and from the friendship as well.

An old adage has it: 'Possession is nine-tenths of ownership!' This could hardly be more incorrect when applied to friendship and love. Yet, too often, our loneliness pushes us to try to possess – and we lose friends precisely to the extent that we give in to this impulse. Thus, we pay a high price if we do not recognise and respond creatively to the pulses that our loneliness sends through us.

Our loneliness often leads us to over-exert ourselves in relationships

Often we try so hard to win people's friendship that the effect is counter-productive and we alienate them from us. There are many examples of this: some of us, for instance, are compulsive talkers. In our efforts to win friendship, we impose ourselves upon others, talking them to death, and tiring and boring them into alienation. Others take the opposite approach and, because they want someone's friendship badly, they avoid that person – hoping of course that their boycott will be noticed and that, by some strange logic, their avoidance of the other person will lead them into friendship. Still others over-exert themselves by becoming what some psychologists call 'pleasers'. A 'pleaser' is a person who, at all costs, continually tries to please others. There is merit in being a 'pleaser', to a degree. However, it is not healthy when the 'pleaser' has to do violence to herself in order to try to please others. In cases like this, she is not being true to herself, nor challenging others as she should. The result is that usually the 'pleaser' ends up losing the respect and genuine friendship of others, and being extremely frustrated and tired as well.[1]

In each of these cases, the root problem is really a failure to come to grips with one's loneliness. Consequently, the loneliness makes us too desperate and we try too hard to win friends. The efforts at friendship are then counter-productive and we end up alienating people from us rather than attracting them to us.

Loneliness can lead us to over-expect within relationships

Unless we understand our loneliness clearly, where it comes from and what it means, we will go through life with the false expectations that somewhere, at some time, someone will be able to take our loneliness away completely. As we shall see later, no relationship , however deep and intimate, can ever fully take our loneliness from us. And, as long as we go through life expecting this, we are doomed to constant disappointment. As well, we will do constant violence to our friendships and love relationships because we will demand from our friends something that they cannot give us, namely, total fulfilment. For example, a goodly number of persons get married precisely because of loneliness. They see their marriage as a panacea for their loneliness. After marriage they discover that they are still lonely; sometimes as lonely as before. Immediately there is the temptation to think that there is something seriously amiss in the marriage, to foist blame on the marriage partner or on oneself, to become disenchanted and seek out new relationships, hoping of course to discover some day the rainbow of total fulfilment. Perhaps there is little amiss with the marriage except the expectations of those within it! Our spiralling divorce rates suggest, among other things, that this syndrome of over-expectation is not uncommon.

Our loneliness, precisely because it is so strong and painful, constantly causes us to look for a 'messiah', that is, for a person who will fully put to rest all the empty spaces inside us. However, no human person can ever completely do that for us. To expect it is unfair. Thus, whenever we enter relationships expecting, not a friend or a marriage partner, but a messiah we do violence to the other and the quality of the friendship and love which is there because we are constantly measuring what we have against an ideal which is not fully realistic in our present human condition.

Loneliness must not be allowed to be an unexamined force within our lives or it will lead us into behaviour which is destructive of love and intimacy.

(2) *Loneliness can prevent us from channelling our creative and affective energies in a meaningful and disciplined way*

All of us go through life wanting to love and wanting to do creative and enriching work. Many of us, though, fare poorly on both counts. Too frequently we do not achieve satisfying love and creative fulfilment. Instead we end up never being able to properly harness and channel our energies for love and work. And so, with our affective and creative energies unbridled, we let ourselves dissipate into mediocrity and frustration.

The colloquial expression, 'Get it all together!' refers precisely to our ability, or lack of it, to get a handle on, and channel creatively, our energies for love and work. Most of us, in fact, never 'get it all together!' Instead we go through life frustrated and dissipated, letting our restless energies push us in one direction, then in another, never quite able to settle down, to figure out what we want to do, and never quite able to discipline ourselves enough to achieve the ends we were meant to attain.

Already back in the fourth century, Gregory of Nyssa wrote about this inability of the human being to 'get it together'. He compares the restless and lonely energies in our heart to a current in a stream:

> Let us imagine a stream flowing from a spring and branching out at random into different channels. Now so long as it flows this way it will be entirely useless for the cultivation of the soul. Its waters are spread out too much; each single channel is small and meager, and the water, because of this, hardly moves. But if we could collect these wanderings and widely scattered channels into one single stream, we would have a full and compact waterflow which would be useful for the many needs of life.

> So too, I think of the human mind. If it spreads itself out in all directions, constantly flowing out and dispersing to whatever pleases the senses, it will never have any notable force in its progress towards the true Good.[2]

This analogy tells us much about why we work and love badly, namely, our restless hearts push us in so many directions that we end up going nowhere.

I want to illustrate this with a modern day parable, the

story of Harry Angstrom, the tragic hero of John Updike's *Rabbit Run*.[3]

Rabbit Run is the story of Harry Angstrom who is called 'Rabbit' by his friends because of his height and his quick nervous gestures. Updike calls him 'rabbit' for more symbolic reasons. As a young boy, Harry is the local high school basketball star. He is also talented in other ways. Intelligent and 'street smart', he is popular with his friends. Yet, Harry is doomed to become a tragic figure. Despite his more than average potential, he never grows or matures.

Harry's problems are many, but at the root of them all is his inability to channel effectively his creative and affective energies, to come to grips responsibly with the lonely forces inside him.

His story starts to take its downhill slide shortly after his high school graduation. Up until then, responsibility and discipline were not required of him, and he fared well. Now when he must take his own life into his hands, the story changes. Bright and capable of going to college, he is too lazy and myopic to take that step. It is easier for him to glory in his past, in his basketball stardom, than to painfully stake out for something new and unknown. He takes a menial job in a local store. As one year breaks into another, and Harry is still at the store, he begins to get frustrated, sensing that he was meant for much more than this. Yet, despite feeling so strongly the frustration of his creative powers, Harry can never read the message that is being spoken to him. He cannot come to grips with the forces inside him and channel them properly. Instead he just lets them bounce him around in all directions, and in no direction in particular. He continues to revel in his past, to live and work in mediocrity, and to fantasise that sooner or later the big break will come and his glory days will return. A man of his talents and abilities will get to the top!

In the meantime he drifts into a marriage. His wife, Janice, not all that different from Harry, challenges him little. As his frustration grows it begins to affect all the areas of his life. He begins to shift the blame for his misfortune away from himself. The world has given me a bad shake! He begins to grow sour, to fantasise more, to live reality less. His marriage deteriorates into passionless boredom which, after a while, can no longer even generate a good hostility. His wife slips into alcoholism, Harry into ennui.

Eventually he runs off. He simply gets into his car one night and drives off, with no particular goal in mind except to get away, leaving behind his pregnant wife and their young son. He takes up with a prostitute and moves in with her.

Some months later, his wife, in a drunken state, accidentally drowns their new baby girl. Harry goes back home for the funeral. It is there that reality hits Harry. Having to face his wife, his friends, his parents and in-laws, and the tragedy of the situation, forces Harry to see the tragedy of his own situation, namely, his own guilt and the real reason for his fouled-up life. Harry sees that he is no longer a promising young man, a star on the way up, shaking off a few bad breaks, but knowing that the rainbow will come. Rather he sees himself as he is in reality, a rather pathetic aging immature boy, a lousy lover living in mediocrity and fantasy, unable to take responsibility for his own life. He realises too that the big break will never come! This realisation is too much for him. The second he senses it all, he runs.

The story ends with Harry running, running away from the funeral of his own child, from responsibility, from his own self!

The book is more than a story, it is a parable. And, as in all parables, we are the central character. We are 'Rabbit' Angstrom. We are the person with the creative and affective energies bubbling inside us. We are the persons cut out to be more than ordinary in this life, the potential star, sure to attain the rainbow. Unfortunately, too, like Harry, most of us do not attain the rainbow. Rather we go through life frustrated and growing sour as we love and work badly, dissipating our energies and accomplishing little. Why?

Mainly because of our inability to understand and come to grips with our own loneliness. Unless our loneliness is understood and handled in a meaningful way, it will never allow us to sweat in lonely solitude and, there, painfully learn the discipline we need to make our love effective and our work creative.

A few other examples will try to further explain how loneliness often dissipates us, causing us to love and work badly:

— *Because of our loneliness we often find it hard to make ourselves present to the moment*

It is not easy to be human. We are so complex. The restless pulses which go through us at each moment make it difficult for us to be free. We are constantly becoming infatuated with certain things, hung up on certain people, nostalgic about certain past friends and moments and caught up in unrealistic daydreams and fantasies. Fraught with this baggage, we are often not free to be fully present to the moment and the people we are experiencing at a given time.

I once met a nun who told me: 'My vocation is, at each moment, to make the person in front of me the most important person in my life!' How few there are who live this vocation! Usually we are in one place, but our hearts are elsewhere.

One of the most frequent complaints one hears today from families, as well as from religious communities, is the complaint: 'We are not spending enough time together!' Few would dispute the validity and importance of this. Yet one cannot help wondering whether the real issue is not the question of psychological presence, rather than mere time spent together. Would the complaint be as frequent if, when families and religious communities actually were together, the members were really present to each other? Even at those times when we are physically together, sharing a meal, a holiday, or a few hours of quiet or television, our minds and hearts are elsewhere and there is no real presence to each other. Rather we all dutifully put in time and put up a façade of presence, while our hearts and fingers fidget, anxiously awaiting the moment when our duty is done and we can finally get to bed, or to the phone, or the car, and to the place where we really want to be.

Lack of presence to the moment also hurts us in other ways. So often we miss out on the richness of life, the beauty of nature, the humour of a moment, or even just the taste of good food, precisely because we are so restless, dissipated, and unfocused that we can neither actualise our presence fully nor capture the moment and what it has to offer us. Life slides by and it is of no great consequence to us whether it is laden with richness and beauty or not since we are too distracted and unpresent to notice. It is for this reason that too frequently our holidays, free time, parties, and social gatherings fail to recreate us in body and mind.

– *Because of our loneliness we find it difficult to make choices*

Many of us find it difficult to make choices. This is not because we cannot find anything that suits our preference, but precisely for the opposite reason, namely, we find it difficult to exclude the things which will not be involved in our choice. Scholastic philosophers had the dictum: 'Every choice is also a renunciation.' Whenever we choose one thing, we necessarily exclude certain other things.

For this reason we find it hard to choose a vocation, an occupation, a set of friends, a life companion, or even a new house or car. The difficulty arises because, in choosing, we have to limit ourselves, and our lonely, insatiable insides rebel against this. Thus, we often end up dissipating our creative and affective energies: hanging loose, spreading ourselves too thin, unable to make clear choices and commitments, procrastinating indefinitely, being wishy-washy, and generally being unable to make decisions which could give our lives more direction and thus help us to love and work more effectively.

—Finally, our loneliness often prevents us from entering into any type of creative solitude

Because we are so lonely and restless, many of us never really attain any inner depth. Rather our loneliness keeps us in a perpetual state of motion and does not allow us to stop our activities long enough to journey inward. Yet this journey is critically important for us.

Artists, poets, philosophers, and religious thinkers of all ages have always challenged us to have within our lives a degree of solitude and interiority. Only by attaining this, do we ever reach our own inner depth and riches. Failure to do it results in superficiality. Catherine de Hueck Doherty, for instance, puts it this way:

> Deserts, silence, solitude. For a soul that realizes the tremendous need of all three, opportunities present themselves in the midst of the congested trappings of all the world's immense cities.

> But how, really, can one achieve such solitude? BY STANDING STILL! Stand still, and allow the strange, deadly restlessness of our tragic age to fall away like the worn-out dusty cloak that it is — a cloak that was once considered beautiful. The restlessness was considered the magic carpet to tomorrow, but now in reality we see it for what it is: a running away from oneself, a turning from that journey inward that all men must undertake to meet God dwelling within the depths of their souls.[4]

Our loneliness, however, often prevents us from making that journey inward. Consequently, many of us end up not attaining our true depth and richness.

(3) *Loneliness can and often does drive us into premature and irresponsible decisions*

Loneliness is one of the most potent forces inside us. This reality is important to recognise since, unless it is dealt with, it can easily become a subconscious tyrant, ruling our lives. This can be bad, especially if it pushes us into premature, ill-thought out, and irresponsible, decisions. A few examples might help to illustrate this.

Many persons, for instance, rush into premature marriages because of loneliness. They believe, perhaps subconsciously, that getting married will take their loneliness away. Often this is disastrous and serves only to intensify the loneliness.

Quite tragically, this is sometimes the case with priests and sisters who leave the priesthood and religious life. Sometimes the decision to leave is a wise one, and for the good of all in the long run. At other times, though, such a decision to leave is too much tied to one's loneliness and one's fantasy of marriage as being the final solution which will take loneliness away. Usually, in cases like these, the decision to leave is not so wise.

Also, and not infrequently, loneliness leads people into dehumanising sexual encounters. A very simple example of this is the person who chooses sexual promiscuity as the lesser of two evils. An illustration might help to clarify what I mean.

A few years ago, while doing graduate work, I served as chaplain in a hostel for young people. Meeting the young people who passed through that house was like attending a seminar on loneliness. One of them was a sixteen-year-old girl whom I shall call 'Becky'.

Becky was a mixed-up young lady. She had been on drugs for nearly two years. She had used everything from LSD to tranquillisers. Lately, she had stopped using hard drugs. Her basic problem was loneliness. She felt friendless and complained bitterly that no one understood her or cared about her. She found no fulfilling friendships either at home, at schools, or within her peer group. She felt lonely and isolated. Drugs had simply been one attempt at somehow filling the void in her life. Her sexual promiscuity had the same aim. She summed up her problem in this area: 'What I need is someone to hold me, to put his arms around me and tell me that I'm important, that I am loved. I crave for that, but I never get it. That's why, at times, I'll go out with guys who I know will take advantage of me. That type of love sure isn't much. I hate myself afterwards, but, anyways, it beats sitting home alone!'

Becky saw her sexual promiscuity as the lesser of two evils. Not all of us are 'Beckys', and not all of us have to face her problems. However, all of us, perhaps in a more sophisticated way, have to make that same type of choice.

Sexuality is not only a powerful instinctual drive within us, but it is, also, radically, the most powerful medium of communication open to human beings. It speaks of totality, of complete encounter. Thus, it is, too, the ultimate temptation in terms of overcoming our loneliness. As we grow more frustrated with the limits and inadequacy of verbal and other means of communication, and find that the dark glass cannot be easily pierced, the temptation is almost automatic: sexual encounter. Surely this type of togetherness will strip away the last barrier that separates us from the other! Surely this will heal our loneliness!

Far too frequently, though, the result does not lead us out of loneliness, but further into it. The issue of intimacy and love, of stripping away the riddle of loneliness cannot be so easily resolved by people simply going to bed with each other. Meaningful love and intimacy, the type which helps rid us of our loneliness, is a complex, hard-to-do, seldom-achieved thing. The history of marital breakups, exploitive relationships, selfish relationships, frustrating relationships, and bitter sour jealous relationships, ending in emptiness, give ample testimony of this. Sexual encounter does not automatically, nor easily, lead to altruism and genuine intimacy. We are flawed, grappling human beings, living in paradox. I believe, with the gospels and with Jesus, that some day this will be overcome and we will all be together in an ecstatic and full sharing – one which includes our total persons, spiritual, psychological, physical, and sexual. Then, and only then will we no longer be living as 'through a glass, darkly', and our loneliness will be fully overcome. That is what, for a large part, the kingdom of God and the body of Christ mean. However, while we wait and work for that final kingdom, we must indeed wrestle with the temptation of needing to touch and be touched, with the tension of our sexuality which so often parades itself as the final solution. And, if our loneliness, be it ever so strong and urgent, causes us to lose patience and try through irresponsible premature sexual encounter to attain togetherness at all costs, then the end result will be counter-productive. The sexual encounter will not generate true intimacy, nor give us respite from our loneliness. Rather it will dehumanise us by weakening our own self-esteem and our respect for others and, thus, lead us further into the riddle of loneliness.[5]

(4) *Loneliness, if it is not faced and grappled with, can lead us to become hardened and desensitised persons*

Loneliness is a pain, and like every pain we suffer it must be listened to and dealt with. For instance, refusal to acknowledge physical pain inside ourselves is very dangerous in that a minor ailment can turn into a serious pathology because it is unattended to. The refusal to acknowledge emotional and psychological pain inside us is equally dangerous. What happens to us when we refuse to listen to the pain of our own loneliness? We become hardened and insensitive persons. This is so because, by refusing to listen to the pain of our hearts, we blunt and harden ourselves to ourselves, to our own real needs and yearnings, and to all that is deepest and softest inside of us. The result is always tragic. Show me a hardened and embittered person, and I will show you a person who has never come to grips with his/her own loneliness!

Again, I would like to illustrate this by means of a modern-day parable. The parable I choose is *The Stone Angel*, by Canadian novelist Margaret Laurence.[6]

The Stone Angel is the story of Hagar Shipley. Hagar herself tells us her story, at age ninety, reflecting back:

She is the daughter of a shop-keeper in a pioneer town on the Canadian prairies. Her father is wealthier and more cultured than most of the other people in that area. Very early in her life, Hagar learns from her father to look with disdain on those less well-to-do, less clear-headed, and weaker than herself. She also learns early in life to look down upon weakness of all kinds, either within herself or within others. The secret of life, as she learns it, is to be self-reliant, independent, never to cry, and to be stronger than others.

As she grows up, goes to an Eastern finishing school, and returns to help her father in his business, Hagar learns more and more how to be in perfect control of herself, how to not feel anything; neither warmth nor sympathy for others, nor weakness, loneliness, nor tears within herself.

Her father considers her too cultured to mix with the local boys, but she rejects her father and eventually marries Bram Shipley, the most uncouth, unmannered, unfeeling, and irreligious man in the area. He is also years her senior. But, alas, Hagar is so unfeeling she does not even seem to notice!

She expects nothing from him (or life) and receives nothing. She is neither happy nor sad, nor depressed or tearful, when her life degenerates progressively into nothing. Worst of all, she is totally uninterested in bettering it. Her father had rejected her when she married Bram, and now, living on his farm out of town, she no longer even goes into town to shop or to go to church. She becomes negligent of her physical appearance, and soon even begins, outwardly, to resemble the ragged Bram. She continues in this way for a meaningless twenty-four years. Then a particular jarring incident moves her to act, and to nearly save herself.

After twenty-four years of semi-comatose existence her physical appearance has degenerated considerably. One day she goes to town with her young son, John, to sell eggs. It is winter and she is dressed particularly shabbily in an old and over-sized parka. She rings a doorbell at a well-to-do house and is greeted by a well-dressed young girl. The young girl calls her mother, saying: 'The egg-woman is here!' The girl's mother turns out to be none other than one of Hagar's former school friends (a person whom Hagar had always disdained and felt superior to). Hagar, hearing herself called 'the egg-woman' by the offspring of her former school friend, is prompted for the first time in years to take a real look at herself. The pain is searing. Immediately upon leaving the house she goes to a public washroom and looks at herself in the mirror. In this one graced moment of clarity she is a mystery to herself:

> I stood for a long time, looking, wondering how a person could change so much and never see it. So gradually it happens . . . The face – a brown and leathery face that wasn't mine. Only the eyes were mine, staring as though to pierce the lying glass and get beneath to some truer image, infinitely distant.[7]

At that moment she makes up her mind to leave her husband. She does this within a few days, taking her son, John, with her. She goes to the West coast, becomes a live-in housekeeper to a well-to-do widower, and slowly regains her manners, cultured speech, and her physical appearance. But in no way does she ever regain her feelings. She lives out her life there as she did with Bram, cold, indifferent, unsympathetic, disdaining the weaknesses of others and those within herself. She suppresses her loneliness, never cries, and never, even for a moment, allows herself to feel genuine warmth or loneliness for another person.

Throughout her life, she experiences moments which open up to the possibility of genuine tenderness. For instance, when her son leaves to go overseas during the war. The moment calls for tenderness, for feeling, but Hagar, as always, manages to close the door just at the moment of opportunity. She refuses to hug her son as he says 'Good-bye':

> I wanted all at once to hold him tightly, plead with him, against all reason and reality not to go. But I did not want to embarrass both of us, nor have him think I'd taken leave of my senses.[8]

This incident is typical of her whole life. That is, at times she almost opens up to genuine warmth, empathy, and tenderness, but always, in the nick of time, caution, hardness, and the necessity of proper appearance take over and prevent her from making the act of abandonment.

As a result she goes through life believing that it is a cruel trick, with really nothing to offer. Her inability to believe in the possibility of meaningful human contact and community also prevents her from believing in God. Her relationship to Him is like her relationship to others and to life in general, namely, a matter of profound indifference. She is agnostic about what life and others have to offer, and thus, logically, she is agnostic about God and what He has to offer.

Her last chance to seize life comes at her death. She is visited, on her deathbed, by her daughter-in-law's minister, and later, by her son.

When he first comes into the room she greets the minister, Mr Troy, with a mixture of pragmatism and indifference. She feels that he has nothing to offer her, but she will be polite so as to get rid of him as easily as possible. He asks her whether he can pray over her. Initially she refuses, but then remembering a church hymn from her youth, she asks him to sing it for her. He consents and begins to sing the hymn. As he sings, the words of the song, coupled with her intuition of her impending death, spark a sensitive moment, a *kairos*:

> 'All people that on earth do dwell,
> Sing to the Lord with joyful voice.'

> I would have wished it. This knowing comes upon me so forcefully, so shatteringly, and with such bitterness as I have never felt before. I must always, always, have wanted that – simply to rejoice. How is it I never could? I know, I know. How long have I known? Or have I always known, in some far crevice of my heart, some cave too deeply buried, too concealed? Every good joy I might have held, in my man or any child of mine or even the plain light of morning, of walking the earth, all were forced to a standstill by some brake of proper appearances – oh, proper to whom? When did I ever speak the heart's truth? Pride was my wilderness, and the demon that led me there was fear. I was alone, never anything else, and never free, for I carried my chains within me, and they spread out from me and shackled all I touched.[9]

However, just as in moments past, Hagar resists redemption. She refuses to cry, to admit guilt, to reach out for help. Instead, after a brief graced moment, she withdraws back into her hardened self and misses redemption as it passes her by. The soil was moist, the rain had come, the sun was warming the fertile land, but she refused to drop the seed.

Her last opportunity for redemptive tears comes hours before her death when her son comes to see her. He lingers by her bedside, awkwardly, and she senses that he wants a final reconciliation with her. (Like Jacob wrestling with the angel: 'I will not let you go before you bless me!') She feigns tenderness and reaches out to him, but underneath her heart remains aloof. She lies to get rid of him, and thus, even on her deathbed is unable to reach a moment of genuine warmth and togetherness. So she dies as she had lived, aloof from life, from herself, her needs, her heart, from others, and from God. Expecting nothing and receiving nothing!

That is the story of Hagar Shipley; a tragedy comparable to any which Shakespeare wrote. In fact Hagar's story is more tragic. In Shakespeare's tragedies, his characters at least die grasping, seeking passion, seeking justice and meaning, seeking love and purpose. Poor Hagar dies seeking nothing, not even death.

On the second page of her autobiography, Hagar describes a gravestone she used to read as a young girl. It read:

Rest in Peace
From toil, surcease,
Regina Weese
  1886

She adds:

So much for sad Regina, now forgotten in Manawaka – as I, Hagar, am doubtless forgotten. And yet I always felt she had only herself to blame, for she was a flimsy, gutless creature, bland as egg custard.[10]

Unfortunately, poor Hagar, too, has only herself to blame for the fact that she too is now forgotten, forgotten because she lived her life devoid of passion, devoid of loneliness or love, devoid of life and God – bland as egg custard!

This story, like Updike's *Rabbit Run*, is also a parable; a painful parable depicting the ultimate hardness of heart, the final sin against the Holy Spirit. Hagar, like millions of us, would not listen to the loneliness and the pain of her own heart. Instead she blunted that voice, hardened herself to its sound, and refused to listen. The result, as is always the result in a case like this, is a desensitised, calloused person, frozen into an incapacity to feel anything, loneliness or love. The result too is a person who is warped to the extent that tears have become impossible for him/her. For such a person, movement towards meaningful life is also impossible for redemption needs human tears in the same way as the flowers of spring need the moisture from the thawed ice of winter.

(5) *Loneliness, if not understood, can be the cause of much inexplicable unhappiness and tension*

Being a human being is not a simple business. Our heart is a caldron full of diverse feelings: restlessness, emptiness, nostalgia, longing, alienation, paranoia, and loneliness. As the caldron is stirred by the events of our lives, these feelings rise to the surface and we find ourselves pushed and pulled in many directions all at the same time. The result, unless it is understood for what it really is, is a painful confusion and tension. This can easily lead to a lot of inexplicable unhappiness as we wonder why we are so restless and divided, and why we cannot simply settle down and be relaxed. Too frequently we worry about this without the aid of proper answers, and this sparks a lot of self-doubts as we wonder whether we are not love-starved, over-sexed, semi-paranoid, and abnormal. A proper understanding of the lonely make-up of the human heart will go a long way in helping us understand that these restless pulses inside may simply indicate that we are emotionally alive and well – and incurably human!

(6) *Ultimately, loneliness can be fully destructive of our human personality*

From the examples given earlier in this chapter, we can see how potentially dangerous loneliness can be. The dangers inherent within loneliness can be summarised by saying that, ultimately, loneliness, if it is not understood and used correctly, can destroy our personality.

Again, I would like to illustrate this by an example; taken from a sixteenth-century writer, John of the Cross.

In his famous treatise, *The Ascent of Mount Carmel*, John outlines a phenomenology of human destruction.[11]

He links it to what he calls 'inordinate affectivity', a phrase which might aptly be translated into 'loneliness gone rampant'. John says that whenever our affectivity becomes inordinate (our loneliness operates without checks) we stand in danger of destroying the very contours of our personality. There are five stages of disintegration in this process of self-destruction:

(i) *We become 'WEARIED AND TIRED'*

If we fail to understand and come to grips with our loneliness, it will inevitably propel us relentlessly into a flurry of activity as we seek to fulfil its demands. And all too often, this is precisely what happens. We bounce from one thing to the next as we try to quench our thirsty unrest. We plunge into a never-ending, but unsatisfying round of parties, socials, drinks, and soul conversations (and, if we can afford it, perhaps psychotherapy as well), as we try to fill a spot in us which will not fill, quench a thirst which will not quench, and satisfy a hunger which will not satisfy.

We do not even know what we want, nor indeed, realise explicitly that we are searching for something. We simply do what comes naturally! We talk, we drink, we do work, we make love, but are dissatisfied, as our human psyche writhes, pulling us this way, then that, leaving us no rest and peace, as we search desperately for someone or something to provide us with completion.

We become like the mythical Greek anti-hero, Sisyphus, who was condemned by the gods to roll a stone up a hill forever. As soon as he got it to the top, the stone rolled back down again, and the unfortunate Sisyphus had to go to the bottom of the hill and roll it back up again. The image is one of frustration, and one of 'weariedness and tiredness'. It is this type of fruitless pursuit that John of the Cross says our loneliness will drive us to, if it is not handled correctly.

(ii) *We become 'TORMENTED AND AFFLICTED'*

If we do not come to grips with our loneliness at the first stage and, like Sisyphus, end up compelled to do fruitless and tiring activity, eventually what will happen is that the tiredness which results from so much frustration will become an abiding pain, like a psychic toothache. The weariness we experience will no longer be intermittent and of the type which can be cured by a good night's sleep or a day off. Rather it will be a weariness whose pain is constant, and which extends into the very marrow of our being. And, if our loneliness remains unchecked, soon the pain will begin doing its real damage.

(iii) *We become 'DARKENED AND BLIND'*

By this, John means that the pain we are experiencing will slowly start to cloud our intellect and understanding. As we know, any strong pain or passion colours our manner of thinking. For example, lust or hatred can cause us to see things from a very different perspective than we normally would. This is what rampant loneliness will eventually do to us. It will fog up our understanding and judgement, causing us to rationalise falsely, to be cynical, and to see things with less than clear understanding.

This leads us to the fourth stage:

(iv) *We become 'DEFILED AND STAINED'*

What is affected at this stage is our aesthetic being. Once our understanding and judgement are impaired, it does not take long before we are no longer a very beautiful person. A person who is falsely rationalising, living in cynicism, constantly complaining, forming unfair judgements, and seeing the world in a negative and distorted way, is not a very beautiful person! Yet this is the extent to which loneliness, if unchecked, will ultimately drive us. And, potentially, it can even drive us further until:

(v) *We become 'WEAKENED AND LUKEWARM'*

By this, John of the Cross refers to our freedom and will power, to our ability to be what we want and to act in a manner true to ourselves. He tells us that if the deterioration process is not checked at the first four levels, eventually our very freedom and personality will be severely impaired, perhaps fully destroyed. What happens is that we end up doing things which are no longer expressive of our true selves. For instance, no one who wakes up in a gutter from too much drink, no one who jumps off a bridge, or no one who alienates all his/her friends through a bitter and cynical attitude, truly wants to be that way. We do those things only when we are no longer capable of doing something else, only at the end of a long process in which we have gradually lost our freedom to be who and what we would like to be. We do those things when our will, for whatever reason, cannot bring us to express ourselves as we really are.

Hence we see that loneliness, if it is not checked, can ultimately be destructive of our very freedom. When this happens, our personalities are effectively destroyed as well since we are powerless to be our own person.

From this, as well as from the other examples, we see how potentially dangerous loneliness can be. However, the dangers are much greater when we refuse to recognise these problems as stemming from loneliness and especially at those times when we lack the honesty to admit that we are indeed lonely, that not all is well with us, and that volcanic forces dwell, not far below the surface, inside us. When, instead, we play games with ourselves and others, masking our real pain and pretending that all is well, when in fact it is not, we slowly build up inside ourselves seething pressures which will eventually work their way to the surface and, there, either cause us some type of breakdown when our defences cave in, or just as tragically, will slowly begin to tire us, to sour our attitudes, to make us less than beautiful, and to destroy our freedom.

Loneliness is not a force to which we can afford to be indifferent. It is of paramount importance, therefore, that we seek to understand it, to find out where it comes from, what it means, and how we can deal with it effectively.

SOME HUMANISTIC SOLUTIONS AND THE NEED FOR A THEOLOGICAL ANSWER

Humanistic approaches

What causes our loneliness? What can take our loneliness away? No one can be indifferent to these questions. Even the failure to respond is itself a response. Loneliness, like all the great existential questions, forces every person to react in some way.

However, until recently there was not an abundance of literature on the matter. But this is not to suggest that great thinkers were not addressing themselves to the problem. Virtually all the great systems of thought, be they political, philosophical, religious, social, or psychological, have taken up the question of loneliness, in some form, and provided some answers to it.

Very often it was not an explicit theme within their works. Nonetheless, all the great systems of thought contain, either explicitly or implicitly, both an anthropology and a soteriology, that is, an understanding of the person and a corresponding theory of how the human being can be brought to fulfilment.

What are some of the answers they have given? Before going into any specifically Christian answer, it is profitable to look at some of the explanations that have been given by people operating outside a specific perspective of faith.

Who are these persons? They are many and have very diverse theories. For purposes of convenience, and at the risk of oversimplification, I have grouped them into two essentially different categories: *humanistic optimists* and *humanistic stoics.*[1]

(1) *Humanistic Optimists*

Under this title, I have grouped a number of diverse thinkers and systems of thought on the basis of a few common denominators. This group is made up of all those who, first of all, view the problem of loneliness from a humanistic rather than from a faith perspective. In addition they are all essentially optimistic about the solutions which we can come up with in terms of handling our loneliness. Hence, they are termed, precisely, Humanistic Optimists.

This group shares another common point: they all believe that human loneliness is in some way caused by conditions within which we live and that the solution to loneliness lies essentially within human powers. However, beyond this common denominator, Humanistic Optimism is made up of many different types of thought. For purposes of analysis, I have divided them into *five* basic groups or ideal types. In a very loose way, I will refer to them as: The 'Marxists', the 'psychotherapists', the 'Marcusians', the 'evolutionists', and the 'naturalists'. Very briefly, here is how each of these groups views the problem of human loneliness.

(i) *The 'Marxists'*

By this term, I want to refer not necessarily to all doctrinaire Marxists, but rather to all those who operate outside a faith perspective and who place the essential blame for human loneliness on the socio-economic-political conditions of society.

'Marxists' generally take up explicitly the question of human loneliness. Most often they call it alienation. They see two interconnected reasons for *alienation*:

First, they attach much of the blame for our alienation to our belief in a God. This belief, they feel, has helped alienate us from ourselves and, consequently, from others. Using Hegelian dialectics they explain this as follows.

Originally when the human person came to full consciousness, the human mind found itself to possess extraordinary qualities of reason and virtue (the Hegelian Thesis). However, at this stage of development, the human species was not yet able to properly accept and handle these qualities. Thus, it projected them outside itself into a concept of a God which we created in our 'image and likeness', (the Hegelian Antithesis). Thus we were fundamentally alienated from ourselves since we, so to speak, ripped out of ourselves many of our best qualities and projected them into a God, leaving ourselves thereby impoverished. The turning-point within human history will come when we negate our concept of God and take back for ourselves those qualities and attributes which we have projected into that concept.

That movement of negation will transform theology into anthropology. 'God' will become man in the true sense and will bring the human species to full maturity. Ultimately, this will make us a species worthy of worship (the Hegelian Synthesis). At this time, too, our fundamental alienation will be largely overcome.[2]

In addition, 'Marxists' see many of our present and past economic, political, and social structures as helping to alienate us from each other. Many of our present institutions and structures, they feel, make it difficult or impossible for the individual to be truly free and hence, unlonely.

For a non-Christian 'Marxist', the solution to human loneliness lies in the human race coming of age, negating its concept of God, and changing the unjust structures and institutions which help alienate us from each other.

(ii) *The 'psychotherapists'*

This title refers simply to all those who would give an essentially psychological explanation to the problem of loneliness.

Despite immense differences among themselves, in essence, this group would all agree that we are lonely because of the psychological difficulties we have in relating to ourselves and to each other in satisfying ways. Different individuals within this group would assign different reasons as to why these difficulties exist. For some, it is because of unresolved instinctual tendencies; for others, it is because of certain traumatic experiences in our past which have left us scarred and ridden with complexes and phobias. For others yet, our problems stem from our inability to sufficiently integrate important experiences into our real self, to cope with our subconscious, or simply from our inability to grow up. However, regardless of the precise factor, or combination of factors, which an individual might assign to explain human alienation, a basic common denominator runs through all individuals within this group. In essence, they all believe that we are lonely because of certain psychological factors which prevent us from relating both to ourselves and to others in a way which is completely wholesome and fulfilling. These difficulties, they believe, can be largely overcome: hypothetically at least, we can be led to grow out of our loneliness.

(iii) *The 'Marcusians'*

By this label, I refer to all those who look for the cause of, and the solution to, our loneliness in both the socio-economic-political conditions and the psychological conditions within which we live. These persons are termed 'Marcusian', after Herbert Marcuse, the great philosopher of our own century, whose genius it was, precisely, to synthesise these two perspectives, namely, the socio-economic-political and the psychological.

This group attempts to come to a more holistic anthropology and soteriology by combining what is best in those who explain our loneliness from a 'Marxist' perspective with what is best in those who explain it from a psychological one. Their explanation of loneliness, and of human problems in general, focuses on both these aspects.

Their precise explanation will vary with the individual who is giving it, but, as in previous groups, a certain common denominator emerges: the human being is lonely and alienated because the socio-economic-political and institutional conditions under which we live do violence to us as persons, ultimately warping our psyches and leaving us unfree and alienated. Certain inherent psychological factors also contribute to our state of bondage. What must be changed in order for us to become more whole, and unlonely, are the conditions which cause this, both the psychological and the socio-economic-political ones.

For instance, here is how one young person who was deeply committed to one of the radical movements in the late nineteen sixties expressed it to me: 'We are committed to political and social action; some of it unlawful and violent. But what we are really aiming at is not so much the political, economic, and social institutions of our society. They are important, but they are not what we are ultimately driving at. What the real issue is, is *how people relate to each other*. That's really what we are out to change. We have to change the fundamental way we relate to each other and strip our relationships of competition and violence which are put there from our earliest youth. You know, from the time we are little kids, we are taught to relate violently and competitively. We are always trying to beat each other, whether it is in the classroom, on the sports field, or in the way we dress, the type of house we live in, the kind of car we drive, or whatever! What happens is that we never learn to relate to each other in non-violent and non-competitive ways. All our relationships are charged with violence. After a while we are no longer free to love each other. It is no wonder we are so alienated and lonely in our society. What we are trying to do is to change the way people relate to each other. Changing the structures is important, but not the real issue.

'And even so, that is still not the whole problem. So much of the difficulty lies within ourselves. It comes from our own hang-ups which seem to be there even before society lays some more on us. I think that everyone should have psychotherapy; otherwise we all go through life as emotional runts!'

This is only one example of this type of approach to the problem of loneliness. There are many other examples. For instance, many of the so-called radical groups of the past decade were motivated, in one fashion or another, by a 'Marcusian' approach. Although they espoused different methods of action and different precise ideologies, underneath there was constantly this common denominator: what is amiss in our human condition, including that which causes our essential loneliness, is a bondage within the human mind, a bondage partly inherent and partly brought on by the socio-economic-political structures of our society. What is needed in terms of a solution is a liberation of all fronts. The structures of society must be changed, our institutions must be changed, and we must rebel metaphysically against the restraints and hang-ups within our own psyches. For our minds to be set free the liberation must be all-inclusive.

(iv) *The 'evolutionists'*

Within this ideal type, I would classify all those who, in one form or another, see progress and development, be it collective or individual, as the ultimate answer to our human problems, including the problem of loneliness. Again, there are within this group many and very diverse persons and systems of thought. However, as in the other groups, there is underneath a common thread unifying all the various approaches. That thread is a faith, expressed or non-expressed, in evolution and the adaptability of the human species. For this group, most human problems, including loneliness, are basically reducible to problems of improper adaptation and underdevelopment. A few examples will help make this clear:

A large number of us live under what might aptly be termed 'the myth of progress': ultimately, though perhaps not expressedly, we believe that most of our problems, including loneliness, would go away if we could ever get ourselves set up in the way we would like to be. We see most of our problems as connected to the fact that we have not yet attained the success in our work, the circle of friends, the prestige and security, and the particular life style we would like. The key phrase here is 'not yet'. The implication is, of course, that some day we will attain those things and then our problems will disappear; at least most of them. Hence, in fact our belief is that ultimately we can outgrow most of our problems. All we need to do is to fit ourselves creatively enough into the web of life.

In the past this type of faith has sometimes taken rather unsophisticated forms. For instance, before the two world wars and many of the other human atrocities of our century, several generations of thinkers, sometimes with incredible crassness, saw within the forces of social, economic, and especially technological development a final solution to our human problems. For them, the answer to nearly all our problems lay in progress, pure and simple. Salvation was reduced to evolution, advancement in technology, and a rise in the standard of living.

Our own century has all but buried the belief that salvation lies simply in technological and economic progress, their importance notwithstanding. They are not the final solution. However, perhaps because of the amount of truth which lies in stressing the importance of development, many still have a basic faith in the belief that some kind of progress is the answer. The form their belief takes is much more sophisticated and nuanced than previous views, but in the end the conclusions are the same, namely, that progress and development are the final solution to our problems.

A recent example of this can be found in Gail Sheehy's bestseller, *Passages*. Despite the many excellent ideas in this book, and despite Sheehy's claim that her analysis is descriptive and not prescriptive,[3] in the end, a prescription for what ails the person does emerge quite clearly. That prescription, taken in its simplest form, is not very different, only more nuanced, than the prescriptions of all 'evolutionists', that is, given sufficient development, the problems will go away. The difference being that, in Sheehy's case, the development spoken about, the myth of progress, is not so much economic or technological as personal. For each of us, sufficient personal development will take care of most of our problems, including loneliness. We can live whole and meaningful lives, beyond alienation, providing that we attain a sufficient degree of personal awareness, honesty, and self-development.

In this belief, Sheehy looks like all 'evolutionists', past and present. Their credo, taken at its lowest common denominator, might be put like this: things are not perfect because we have not yet advanced far enough. However, present difficulties, including the problem of loneliness, can potentially be worked through and surmounted.

(v) The 'naturalists'

The final group which offers an ideal type analysis and solution is a group who might aptly be called the 'naturalists'. What is common to them is the belief that most of our essential and existential problems, including alienation, stem from the fact that we have distorted and warped our proper relationship to the physical universe. The solution to our problems, then, lies in restoring our proper relationship to nature. Salvation is very much tied to understanding and respecting nature.

In its most serious forms, this type of approach contains considerable depth and challenge. It points out to us the deep alienation that can result from losing our proper connection to nature. We see examples of this, for instance, in many recent writings which point out to us the alienation that results when we sever our proper relationship to our own bodies by viewing them platonically or Manichaeistically. As well, ecologists, health food people, and poets are constantly making us aware of our vital link to nature. Their emphases may be different, but their message has a marked unanimity.

Also, few of us who have read John Steinbeck's *The Grapes of Wrath*, can ever forget some of his poignant passages describing the alienation which results from losing our proper connection with nature; in this case, with the soil which produces the bread we eat. In one particularly powerful passage, Steinbeck puts his whole message into one image as he describes a tractor ploughing up farm land. The image becomes powerful when we understand the background to it.

The drought of the nineteen thirties was forcing many small farmers in the mid-west to give up their lands to pay the debts which they owed to the bank which is always presented as being anonymous, a force which nobody owned and seemed responsible for. No one even seemed to know where it was located, or who issued its orders. People were only aware that they owed to the bank, that the bank was demanding their land, and that the bank was driving them off. As the bank seizes their land, and one by one the farmers leave the soil they so dearly love, despite the hard times, they turn to look back as a massive iron tractor, the symbol of progress, comes to plough up their lands. Old boundaries, old houses, old farming methods, and an old way of life all crumple before the massive iron tractor, progress, as it does its work – in straight lines! And it works for the bank, that ultimate unknown force! Steinbeck, in a powerful passage, describes the tractor operator, the driver of progress:

The man sitting in the iron seat did not look like a man; gloved, goggled, rubber dust mask over nose and mouth, he was a part of the monster, a robot in the seat. The thunder of the cylinders sounded through the country, became one with the air and the earth, so that earth and air muttered in sympathetic vibration. The driver could not control it – straight across country it went, cutting through a dozen farms and straight back. A twitch at the controls could swerve the cat, but the driver's hands could not twitch because the monster that built the tractor, the monster that sent the tractor out, had somehow got into the driver's hands, into his brain and muscle, had goggled and muzzled him – goggled his mind, muzzled his speech, goggled his perception, muzzled his protest. He could not see the land as it was, he could not smell the land as it smelled; his feet did not stamp the clods or feel the warmth and power of the earth. He sat on an iron seat and stepped on iron pedals. He could not cheer or beat or curse or encourage the extension of his power, and because of this he could not cheer or whip or curse or encourage himself. He did not know or own or trust or beseech the land. If a seed dropped did not germinate, it was nothing. If the young thrusting plant withered, in drought or drowned in a flood of rain it was no more to the driver than to the tractor.

He loved the land no more than the bank loved the land. He could admire the tractor – its machined surfaces, its surge of power, the roar of its detonating cylinders; but it was not his tractor. Behind the tractor rolled the shining disks, cutting the earth with blades – not plowing but surgery, pushing the cut earth to the right where the second row of disks cut it and pushed it to the left; slicing blades shining, polished by the cut earth. And pulled behind the disks, the harrows combining with iron teeth so that the little clods broke up and the earth lay smooth. Behind the harrows, the long seeders – twelve curved iron peens erected a foundry, orgasms set by gears, raping methodically, raping without passion. The driver sat in his iron seat and he was proud of the straight lines he did not will, proud of the tractor he did not own or love, proud of the power he could not control. And when that crop grew, and was harvested, no man had crumpled a hot clod in his fingers and let the earth sift past his fingertips. No man had touched the seed, or lusted for the growth.

Man ate what they had not raised, had no connection with the bread. The land bore under iron, and under iron gradually died; for it was not loved or hated, it had no prayers or curses.[4]

Obviously by this image, Steinbeck hints at much more than the importance of a proper relationship to nature. However, what he does say about that relationship should not be denigrated.

Human loneliness is a tremendously complex, many-faceted phenomenon. Clearly, a proper relationship to nature does play a role in determining how lonely we will be. Others who have written on this point with much depth and sensitivity include Jacques Cousteau, Rachel Carson, and Loren Eiseley.[5]

These, in an extremely sketchy fashion, are some of the perspectives that Humanistic Optimism sheds on the problem of loneliness. Obviously there is considerable depth and truth to each of these positions. Many of their perspectives will be taken up again in Part Two of this book when we will look at ways of handling loneliness creatively. However, as will also be shown later, these perspectives, if taken by themselves, are not enough to fully understand or deal with the problem of loneliness. The lonely pains which gnaw at the human heart will only be fully placated by a deeper answer.

(2) *Humanistic Stoics*

Designated by this title are all those thinkers and systems of thought who view the problem of loneliness from a humanistic perspective but, unlike their optimistic counterparts, see no real solution to the problem. Although there are really millions of people who feel this way, not all are able to articulate their pessimism regarding the problem of loneliness. The clearest and most articulate expressions of this type of approach can be seen in the writings of many of the great existential philosophers and poets of our century. Men such as Albert Camus, Jean-Paul Sartre, and Martin Heidegger have written at length on this issue. For them, as for millions of others less articulate, the problem of human loneliness is really one for which there is no answer, or, at best, only a partial answer. They all agree that there is something amiss within the human condition. However, for them, the real pathos or canker is the human condition itself. The basic problem, as they see it, is that we are not built for the type of world we live in. We are beings with unlimited dreams and ideals, and insatiable yearnings. But we live in a world which is small and petty, shot through with limitedness at every turn, and which chokes us off on every side. We are extraordinary beings living in an all too ordinary world. We simply are not at home!

Albert Camus, in his book *The Fall*, uses the stark image of a medieval prison to portray this. In some medieval prisons the cell was constructed in such a way that the man in it could never stretch out to his full height, either when standing up or lying down. The person had always to be stooped or curled up. The rationale behind this was that those who built the prison believed that if the person could never straighten up (the 'box' was always too small for him) eventually this would break his rebellious spirit. Camus uses this as an analogy to throw light on our relationship to the world: The world is a 'box' which is too small, too limited to contain us. We can never straighten up completely, to our full height. The longer we live this way the more hunch-backed, lonely, we become.[6]

For this group there is no real answer to loneliness, except the answer of Stoicism. Since we are unsuited for this world ('we are verses out of rhythm, couplets out of rhyme') and our loneliness stems from that, our only answer is to accept loneliness, face it with honesty, and look for those few principles that will help calm the infinite anguish of our free spirits. Moreover, if loneliness is accepted in this honest way, it can be beneficial to us. For though ultimately irremediable, it can be for all of us lonely individuals, the thread which binds us together in empathy and purpose. Loneliness, if faced honestly, can motivate us to rebel against the absurdities and pain which seem so omnipresent within the world.

Humanistic Stoicism, as is evident from even so brief a

sketch, offers a very sensitive analysis of human loneliness, with both its pains and its potential value. However, in the end, as does all Stoicism, it falls short of providing a fully satisfying answer. What it says is valuable and good. Yet, somehow, the human heart demands that there be something more.

The need for a theological answer

We began this chapter with two questions: What causes loneliness? What can take our loneliness away? Humanism, as we can see, has much to offer us vis-à-vis both these questions. However, as will become clearer when we analyse human loneliness, there are aspects to human loneliness which will admit no adequate answer outside a faith perspective. For even if all pejorative conditions within our world were remedied we would still be lonely. From a humanistic perspective alone will never come a fully satisfying answer to the question of loneliness. Humanistic Stoicism itself admits this. The lonely thirst raging within the heart will not be easily nor quickly quenched. A theological answer, the living waters promised by the gospels, is needed.

Hence the real task of giving us a liberating answer to the problem of loneliness belongs to theology. Unfortunately, theology, with its privileged access to revealed truth, has not always addressed itself to this task. For instance, as yet, nothing resembling a really comprehensive work on the theology of loneliness has appeared. While the problem has prompted a wealth of literature in other fields (sociology, psychology, philosophy, medicine, and poetry), the theological bookshelves display only partial treatises on the issue; though, admittedly, some of these are excellent.[7]

The fact that so much theology has failed to address itself explicitly and systematically to this problem is unfortunate for, by this failure, theology abdicates one of its true functions and, at the same time, stands indicted by the perennial critique of those who accuse theology, precisely, of not being attuned to real life.

The task of theology, of any theology, must always be first and foremost to form a vision of God. That is of paramount importance. However, in forming this vision of God, theology (and the theologian) must come to understand God in such a way that this understanding has consequences in real life. Thus, any worthwhile theology must, at a certain point, bring its vision of God to bear upon the actual, and very specific, problems which are gripping people's lives.[8] All good theology must, in a sense, be liberation theology.

An excellent paradigm for a method in theology can be taken from the so-called liberation theologies of South American theologians.[9] Liberation theology sees the primary function of theological reflection as not being so much for the purpose of 'saving souls' for the next life, nor of doing apologetics (to make ourselves credible to non-Christians and Christians of other denominations), nor indeed of simply clarifying and honing the tradition ('art for art's sake'). These functions, however valid in themselves, are not the primary task of theology. In the end, theology is not primarily intended to offer perspectives on a life beyond, nor to try to persuade other people that we are credible, nor to be an art form to please theological aesthetes. The real task of theological reflection is rather to bring a vision of God to bear upon life in such a way that the persons who share that vision are freed to really live life, this life and the next one, as God intended it.

For theology to achieve this, the liberation theologians see the necessity of it being an interplay of three moments:

(i) **an analysis of reality:** it must include a critical and systematic analysis of our lived experience.

(ii) **theological reflection on that situation:** a vision of God must be brought to bear on that specific situation.

(iii) **a return to the situation:** personal and pastoral consequences, actually affecting life, must flow logically from the theological reflection.

Thus, for example, many South American theologians focus on the oppression of the poor and underprivileged in their countries. They then try to bring a vision of God to speak to that situation. Logically, this leads to a certain critique of the situation and, as well, to certain pastoral and personal consequences vis-à-vis that specific situation of oppression. Ultimately, and hopefully, this reflection provides the understanding and the vision needed to move in the direction of liberation from the oppressed situation.

I have made this brief excursion on method in theology, and the method of liberation theology in particular, because it is my belief that, today, the forces of loneliness and restlessness enslave us, violently and radically. Just as any oppressed people needs to be liberated, we too need to be liberated. For we too live in a 'totalitarian' state, oppressed. The loneliness of our heart dictates with absoluteness. We are an unfree people, oppressed from within and without.

More than three thousand years ago, the Jewish people found themselves enslaved in Egypt. As their pain grew daily, they began to cry to a God, whose name they did not yet know, to save them, to set them free. A God, Yahweh, heard their groaning and prayers. He sent them a liberator to lead them out of their oppression to the promised land. Since that time, millions of others, enslaved and poor, have looked at their abject state and called to Yahweh for help, for liberation. We stand in that tradition. And, like the millions before us, we too need to cry to Yahweh, for a Moses, a Liberator, for understanding, for grace, for patience, for all those things it will take to lead us out of the slavery of loneliness, out of that damned aloneness, and into the promised land!

BRINGING THE PROBLEM INTO THEOLOGICAL FOCUS: THE TYPES OF LONELINESS

The need for a definition

How are we to be led out of the slavery of loneliness? How are we to pierce the riddle of loneliness, and move beyond living as through a glass, darkly? Before even attempting to take up this question meaningfully, it is necessary to define loneliness more exactly. Loneliness is not a monolithic phenomenon. As we shall see, there are different types of loneliness, stemming from different causes, having different meanings, and requiring very different solutions. Some types are important, others are not; some types have a theological root, others do not; some types can be a sign of health, others not; and some types are ephemeral, and others are not. Before going any further it is necessary to differentiate among them.

What is loneliness? Nearly all analysts see the futility of trying to define it in any dictionary-type fashion. There can be no simple definition of loneliness. What is more useful is to divide it into various categories or types. For example, Rubin Gotesky[1] does a serious phenomenological study of loneliness and concludes by distinguishing among what he calls *aloneness*, *loneliness*, and *solitude*. Usually we apply the one term, loneliness, to all three of these. This is somewhat of an equivocation. For Gotesky, *aloneness* denotes a simple spatial separation from other people which, in terms of feeling, is neutral. It is neither necessarily painful nor pleasant, but is simply the fact of being alone. *Loneliness*, on the other hand, is precisely a painful experience, the feeling which results when we are separated from others in such a way that we feel excluded, rejected, or involuntarily cut off. *Solitude* is the state of being alone, but being serene and peaceful in that state.

That is just one example of this type of analysis. There are many others,[2] each having its own particular usefulness. There is not one normative analysis or definition of loneliness. Different analyses produce different kinds of categories, all of them valid in themselves, and all of them useful in different ways. For my own purposes it has been most useful to divide loneliness into *five* types.[3] However, before outlining these types, a brief general definition of loneliness is in order.

A general definition

Loneliness is an experiential reality. Like other experiential realities such as joy, sorrow, and freedom, it affects not just our intellects, but our emotions and even our bodies. Thus, it is first and foremost an experience of our whole person.

What is this experience? At a certain level it is inchoate, an undifferentiated mixture of feelings of alienation, exclusion, rejection, longing, discontent, restlessness, emptiness, frustration, dissatisfaction, incompleteness, insatiability, nostalgia, and death. At this level, too, these feelings are often not yet clearly directed towards any specific object. We just feel lonely! However, all these feelings do have an object. For example, we always long for something or someone; we are frustrated about something; or we are incomplete for some reason.

What is the object of our various feelings of loneliness? To attempt any type of exhaustive listing would be impossible since nearly every human feeling we have has some dimension of loneliness to it. Only in the concrete, when we are confronted with this or that particular feeling of loneliness, can we sometimes pinpoint a precise object towards which our loneliness is directed. Since there can be no complete list of all the various feelings of loneliness with their corresponding objects, we can only look at a certain sampling.

What are we lonely for? We are lonely for many things: we are lonely for more love and communication, more unity and understanding, than we have at present. We are longing and restless for a wholeness we do not yet possess. We are tormented by feelings of insatiability, thirsting constantly, wanting to know more people, wanting to be known by more people, wanting to be in more places, and wanting to be 'where it is at', in every sense of that cliché. We are frustrated because our relationships are too frequently fraught with ambiguity and misunderstanding, with pettiness and betrayal. We feel empty and incomplete because we are missing out on so much of life, constantly living at the fringes, as behind a glass, darkly, away from the action, unable to completely sort through the riddle of life, at the door without a key, unable to fully enter. We feel nostalgia and death as precious friends and precious moments leave us, never to return, as youth and fullness slowly leave our bodies, as the clock ticks away and we lose so much of what we have had. We feel both agony and ecstasy in our loneliness as we experience both the tension which makes for life and the loss which makes for death.

Specific types of loneliness

Beyond this general definition, loneliness can be divided into various kinds. For purposes of analysis in general, and theological analysis in particular, I wish to divide loneliness into *five* types, which I call: 'alienation-loneliness', 'restlessness-loneliness', 'fantasy-loneliness'. 'rootlessness-loneliness', and 'blues-loneliness'. Since they are types, they are not always and everywhere distinct from each other. There is some overlapping but, as will be shown, there is a clear distinction among them, one which can be drawn on the basis of their cause, their meaning, and their resolution.

(1) 'Alienation-loneliness'

'Alienation-loneliness' is the easiest type of loneliness to understand. It is what most people mean when they use the word loneliness. It refers simply to the experience of feeling alienated or estranged from others. It is the feeling we have when we are not able to love and understand, and be loved and understood, as fully as we would like, or as fully as we should as human beings. When our relationships are inadequate to the point of being painful and frustrating to us, we suffer 'alienation-loneliness'.

Many factors cause 'alienation-loneliness', for example, fear, shame, lack of self-esteem, paranoia, ideological differences with others, selfishness, fear of rejection by others, positive rejection by others, physical handicaps, emotional handicaps, physical separation from others, or anything else which hinders us from relating as closely and intimately to others as we would like. In addition, as we saw in Chapter 1, today a number of cultural factors, such as impersonalisation, increased mobility, future shock, and the movement towards increased privacy, are potential causes of this type of alienation.

We are social beings, meant to live in love and intimacy with others. Our nature demands this. When, for whatever reasons, we cannot achieve this, and communicate and love as we should, then something is missing inside us – and we feel it! We feel estranged and alienated.

'Alienation-loneliness', like its counterparts, can best be understood by examining an example of its extreme form. As a 'classic' example of this type of loneliness, I quote, in full, a letter which was recently given me by the principal of a large high school. A few days earlier, he had delivered his beginning-of-the-year address to the entire student body. He had concluded his address with the phrase: 'I hope you will be happy and gain a worthwhile education here.' Several days later he found this letter under his office door.

Dear Mr————:

Hello! I am a grade 11 (male) student at this school. I want to type you a letter and give you and the other teachers a little idea of what I (and some others maybe) have to put up with! I don't think other students are getting the same treatment that I am getting. I hope you will read my letter and think about it, if you truly mean what you said in your address: 'I hope you will be happy and gain a worthwhile education here.'

I have been harassed and bugged since grade 7. I see no reason for why the students should bug me, but I really get bugged heavily all the time. You would not believe how much I get bugged. Everyone bugs me, all the grades and all the students. I am called names such as 'fagot' and 'homosexual', etc. I am not any of those things and cannot take much more of this harassment. I try to ignore it or not let it bother me but I am sensitive and it really bothers me! I get bugged a real lot and the teachers don't seem to stop the students from doing it. I am seeing our family physician every 2 weeks and also a psychiatrist every week concerning paranoia. I am becoming paranoid and very self-conscious because of this happening at school. I am not crazy but I am getting very upset and emotional because of all of this. I am not ugly, I am not bad-looking and I get along okay with others. But no one will be my friend as they don't want to be involved etc. . . . It is important to have a boy-girl relationship, but it is impossible for me as I am being bugged so much. I am not exaggerating. And all this is affecting my study habits etc. and it affects me all over.

Last year my mother and I saw one of the teachers regarding this matter and nothing was really done. I realize that you can't stop this but you could tell the teachers to stress better kindness towards others. Especially the religion teachers. I thought this was supposed to be a catholic school!

I do not intend to go to the grade 12 graduation this year or next and I have never gone to any dances also because of getting bugged by everyone.

I am really getting to the point where I can't take anymore of this. My doctor has given me some tranquilizers to make me not so tense and emotional so I can study and work better. I wish that you and the other teachers would realize what I am going through! (Maybe others too!)

I hope you will show this to the teachers or mention it at least. I hope this makes you a little more aware of what is going on in our school. I hope the teachers will stress the point about being kind to others. Please tell them not to mention this letter though as some of the kids might think I wrote it. Please make sure the students don't know about this letter. I am depressed all day about this. I know that you really can't stop it but you could help.

I hope you understand me and I hope you are not mad that I wrote this letter. I am sorry if I took a lot of your time.

I am looking forward to this year, but I am hoping it will be better for me.

Thank-you for your time!

Grade 11 (male) student.

That is one example of 'alienation-loneliness'. There are many others: the *deaf-mute*, struggling to communicate; the *abused child*, who grows up bitter and resentful, unable to love; *the unattractive girl*, unable to get a date, soon shackled by a bad self-image and a shame which leaves her unfree; *the elderly person*, neglected and ignored, shunted off to die alone in a nursing home; *the emotionally scarred person*, living within a protective shell, unable to risk venturing out; *the foreigner*, the object of racial prejudice, struggling to be accepted; *the fat kid*, teased and picked on in the playground; *the poet-dreamer*, misunderstood, and unable to fully share her depth with others. All of these are examples of 'alienation-loneliness' in an intense form.

However, 'alienation-loneliness' does not just strike persons like these. Ultimately it affects all of us to some degree. Everyone is alienated; some more, some less. In extreme cases a person can be so badly alienated that he or she needs professional help. Usually, though, it is a question of pain and frustration being present in our lives because of the inadequacy of our interpersonal relationships.

Also, it is important to notice that 'alienation-loneliness' is always caused by certain human factors and is always at least somewhat pathological. Unlike some forms of 'restlessness-loneliness', 'alienation-loneliness' is never a healthy state. Since it is caused by human factors, it can, hypothetically, be overcome if deviant conditions are rectified.

(2) 'Restlessness-loneliness'

'Restlessness-loneliness' is another type of loneliness, which refers not so directly to the experience of alienation or estrangement from others, but to the constant dissatisfaction and restlessness within us which perpetually keeps us frustrated and in a state of unrest. As we shall see too, this type of loneliness is not caused directly by our alienation from others, but from the very way our hearts are built, from our structure as human beings.

All of us experience within ourselves a certain restlessness and insatiability. Our hearts and minds are so fashioned that they are never satisfied, always restless; never quiet, always wanting more of everything. Throughout history various persons have given different names to this restlessness. *Religious thinkers* have often called it 'the spark of the divine to us'; *philosophers* sometimes referred to it as 'the desire of the part to return to the whole'; *the Greeks* had two names for it, *nostos*, a certain homesickness within the human heart, and *eros*, a relentless erotic pull towards whatever we perceive as good; *the Vikings* called it 'wanderlust', the constant urge to explore beyond all known horizons; the biblical writer of Ecclesiastes, *Qoheleth*, called it 'timelessness' (*ha olam*), the congenital inability to bring ourselves into peaceful harmony with the world around us; *St Augustine* called it 'restlessness' – 'You have made us for Yourself, Lord, and our hearts are restless until they rest in you.'[4] Most of us simply call it 'loneliness'.

Whatever name we assign this feeling, the experience is universal. None of us are exempt. Prescinding from more direct feelings of alienation and estrangement, all of us still experience within ourselves a certain lonely thirst. At the centre of our being an insatiable burning pushes us outward in wanderlust and eros, in restlessness and desire, to pursue some unknown timelessness, infinity, and wholeness.

Again, this is best understood when illustrated with some examples. A 'classic' example of this is 'Richard Cory', the tragic hero of Edwin Arlington Robinson's poem.[5] Richard is indeed 'the man with everything', material wealth, fame and prestige, culture and good friends. Yet for a reason which is total mystery to all except to the complexities of the human heart, he goes home one night and puts a bullet through his head. We are all potentially 'Richard Corys' because all of us possess his insatiable heart. The more we have, the more we want!

I wish to offer, by way of illustration, a series of quotes which give 'classic' expression to this experience of 'restlessness-loneliness'. These quotes are taken from a very wide range of persons, living in different times and places, with different backgrounds and beliefs. Yet they all express a common experience, the experience of 'restlessness-loneliness'. From Qoheleth, the enigmatic sage of the Old Testament, from St Augustine, a fourth-century theologian, from a contemporary atheistic philosopher, from a contemporary Christian philosopher, from a sixteen-year-old high school student from Saskatchewan's prairies, and from a famous Swedish film maker, issue forth poignant expressions of this painful experience.

Atheistic French philosopher Albert Camus puts it this way:

I was at ease in everything to be sure, but at the same time satisfied with nothing. Each joy made me desire another. I went from festivity to festivity. On occasion I danced for nights on end, ever madder about people and life. At times, late on those nights when dancing, the slight intoxication, my wild enthusiasm, everyone's violent unrestraint would fill me with a tired and overwhelmed rapture, it would seem to me – at the breaking point of fatigue and for a second's flash – that at last I understood the secret of creatures of the world. But my fatigue would disappear the next day, and with it the secret . . .[6]

What Camus says here echoes what both St Augustine and Qoheleth expressed centuries before him.

You have made us for Yourself, Lord, and our hearts are restless until they rest in You.[7]

He (God) has made everything beautiful in its time; *also he has put timelessness into man's mind,* yet so that he cannot find out what God has done from the beginning to the end.[8]

This bears a marked resemblance to the pain expressed by a sixteen-year-old high school student who writes:

. . . just now I feel like crying, really it's funny, life is so beautiful and I want other people to enjoy it with me. It's funny *here I am with almost everything a person could want and it's not enough. I always want more, no matter what it is.* I keep asking people about it, but, nothing, I get no answers. I don't get it. I feel like jumping for joy sometimes and then, like now, I feel like sitting down and crying my eyes out, but why?[9]

Her problem, in fact, has an answer. Belgian philosopher, Joseph Marechal, albeit in a very abstract way, addresses himself to her question, and says much about loneliness and human nature in general at the same time:

The human intelligence is not merely a mirror passively reflecting the objects which pass within its field, but an activity directed in its deepest manifestations towards a well-defined term, the only term which can completely absorb it – Absolute Being, Absolute Truth and Goodness. The Absolute has set its mark on the basic tendency of our intelligence; moreover, this tendency constantly surpasses the particular acts of the intellect; the mind is driven by its internal dynamism from intellection to intellection, from object to object: but so long as it gravitates in the sphere of the finite, it attempts in vain to liken itself to its internal movement, to rest in the fullness of its act, to affirm Being, by identity, purely and integrally . . . The affirmation of reality . . . is nothing else than the expression of the fundamental tendency of the mind to unification in and with the Absolute.[10]

My final quotation is taken from the Swedish film maker, Ingmar Bergman, and needs some introduction. A few years ago, Bergman released a film entitled *Face to Face*, the story of a lady psychiatrist who is presented as being a well adjusted, intelligent and disciplined person. Comfortably married to a gifted colleague, she is respected in her profession and is surrounded by what is called 'the good things of life'. The film presents her attempt at suicide and her subsequent search for a reason to continue to live meaningfully. She is a person with everything, except a peaceful heart. Before beginning the filming of this movie, Bergman wrote a letter to his cast and crew, telling them the reasons for the film and its importance to him. The following is an excerpt from that letter:

Faro, Sweden

Dear Fellow Workers:

We're now going to make a film which, in a way, is about an attempted suicide. Actually it deals ('as usual' I was about to say!) with Life, Love and Death. The reason is that nothing in fact is more important. To occupy oneself with. To think of. To worry over. To be happy about. And so on.

If some honest person were to ask me honestly just why I have written this film, I to be honest, could not give a clear-cut answer. I think that for some time now I have been living with an anxiety which has had no tangible cause. It has been like having a toothache, without the conscientious dentist having been able to find anything wrong with the tooth or with the person as a whole. After having given my anxiety various labels, each less convincing than the other, I decided to begin investigating more methodically.[11]

Several years ago, Richard Bach wrote a little story about a bird called Jonathan Livingston Seagull.[12] The book struck a resounding chord in the hearts of millions of people. The story is very simple: Jonathan is a gull who is not satisfied with being a gull. Driven by an inexplicable restlessness and a desire for a freedom and a transcendence that he, himself, cannot fully understand, Jonathan wants always to fly higher, fly faster, and fly further than he or any other gull has ever flown. The force in him is relentless, he can find no lasting peace or relaxation as he relentlessly pushes, always straining to break out of the narrow limits within which he finds himself.

This book's astounding popularity testifies to Bach's original hunch that there is a good amount of Jonathan Livingston Seagull in each of us. Everyone identifies with Jonathan. We are that gull, restless and dissatisfied, driven by a perpetual inner disquiet which we do not always fully recognise or understand, pushing, always harder, to fly faster, to go more places, to break through, to break out of the asphyxiating confines of our place and condition in time and history. Jonathan's loneliness is our loneliness. And our loneliness is a 'restlessness-loneliness'.

This type of loneliness does not just affect those persons who have special relational problems. In fact, the reverse appears to be true, namely, the more 'normal' and sensitive a person is, the more likely it is that he/she will suffer from this type of loneliness. For example, it is no secret that many of the world's greatest artists, poets, musicians, philosophers, writers, and creative and sensitive people in general, suffer greatly from this.[13]

How this 'restlessness-loneliness' differs from 'alienation-loneliness' becomes more clear if we compare the loneliness expressed by the two students whose letters we quoted earlier. Both are complaining of loneliness, but what a difference between the types of loneliness of which they complain! In the case of the young man who wrote the letter to his high school principal, the complaint is that he has no friends, no deep relationships, that he is picked on, and feels rejected by others. This is hardly the case with the young lady who wrote the other letter. She is a popular girl, attractive, with many close friends and a loving family. By her own admission, she has 'almost everything a person could want', but by her own admission too, 'it's not enough!' She is still lonely.

In looking at these cases it is critical to distinguish between various types of loneliness. They are both complaining of loneliness but their loneliness is very different, in cause, in meaning, and in resolution. His loneliness suggests a lack of close relationships, hers does not; his loneliness is a very unhealthy state, hers might be indicative of emotional health and sensitivity; his loneliness can be largely resolved by moving out of himself into friendships and activity; hers might require precisely the opposite movement, namely, a slowdown of external activity and a journey inward.

(3) 'Fantasy-loneliness'

The third type of loneliness might aptly be called 'fantasy-loneliness.' It is the loneliness which is caused by our failure to be completely in contact with truth, reality as it is in itself.

Scholastic philosophers define truth as the 'correspondence between what is in the mind, with reality the way it is outside of the mind'. ('Adequatio intellectus et rei.')[14]

They believe that we attain truth, and live in truth, when our thoughts correspond to the way reality is in itself. Conversely, when there is a discrepancy between the two, mind and reality, we suffer illusion, fantasy, or error. For instance, persons seeing a mirage might sincerely believe that they are seeing a lake in the distance, but since there is no correspondence between their thoughts and the actual reality, they are said to be in error. Conversely, if they believe in their minds that trees have roots beneath the ground, albeit not visible, they are said to have attained truth. The idea in their minds corresponds to reality.

Now all of us, according to degree, live in fantasy and illusion, not quite fully in tune with reality. We live with certain fantasies and illusions of who we are and where we fit into reality. We daydream, and after a while, get part of our dreams and fantasies mixed into how we see and interpret reality. Sometimes our assessment of ourselves and our place in life is close to reality; at other times it is fraught with illusion and unreality. To the degree that we are not truly and totally in touch with reality as it is, we are alienated and lonely.

For instance, we all live out various fantasies of ourselves. In our minds we see ourselves as an 'intellectual', a 'mystic', a 'searcher', a 'poet', a 'holy person', an 'indispensable executive', a 'crucial member of the organisation', or as 'your basic nice guy', to name just a few of the more common types. Usually there is a certain amount of truth to it, and we actually possess some of the qualities that we see in our ideal or fantasy of ourselves. However, generally, there is also a discrepancy, at times painfully obvious to others, between our fantasy of ourselves and our true selves.

All of us, I am sure, have the painful experience of living with people whose fantasies about themselves are out of tune with reality. (And others have the 'pleasure' of living with us and our fantasies!) All too common is the so-called 'intellectual', who is really superficial and a put-on; the 'pseudo-mystic', who actually knows little about God or prayer, or anything else; the self-styled 'nice guy', who is nice to everyone except the people he lives with and who have primary claims to his affections; the 'saintly person', who is a miserable specimen of humanity and a purgatory to all around him; the 'crucial member of the organisation', with prestige, a high salary, and little to do, except bear the resentment of those who do the actual work; and the 'poor humble simple soul', whose passive (but very real) aggressiveness is a source of confusion and anger to all around her. All of these persons are out of contact with reality, 'spaced-out', as our modern terminology would put it. All of them are, as well, lonely, partly alienated from the world, from others, and from themselves; alienated by their own fantasy. Failure to live truth causes a type of loneliness. And we all suffer from this type of loneliness, because we all (this side of heaven) live somewhat in fantasy. It is merely a question of degree.

'Fantasy-loneliness', like its counterparts, can be most easily understood by its extreme forms. For instance, a psychotic person can be so out of touch with reality that he imagines himself to be another person, such as Julius Caesar or Napoleon. Or, a young person tripped out on drugs might sincerely feel that he is undergoing profound and important mystical experiences. In both these cases, as well as in the less extreme cases mentioned earlier, we see a discrepancy between the person's state of mind (his fantasy of himself) and the reality (the ontological realities which are operative). In each case the result is loneliness, 'fantasy-loneliness', a losing of contact with others, with God, and with reality, and a slipping further into imprisonment within the lonely confines of one's own mind.

Ralph McInerny, in a novel called *Gate of Heaven*, gives a clear example of this type of loneliness. The story, set within a retirement home for priests, presents an aged and retired Father Stokes who spends his days going to the local airport and having himself paged over the public address system. However, his reason for this is not that he feels any particular thrill in hearing his name announced in a crowded airport terminal, but because of his fantasy that maybe, just maybe . . .

Stokes was not in his room. After the visit to the Founder's bedside he had put on his coat and walked away from Porta Coeli. He did not like to take a nap. He slept poorly enough at night without coddling his body during the day. He walked around the lake and across campus, ignored by the young, ignoring them, to the bus stop. Downtown he transferred and took a number 36 to the airport. It was a favorite spot. He went up to the observation platform and looked over the field . . .

A commercial jet approached from the east, most likely from Cleveland. Stokes leaned on the railing and watched it come down, tons and tons of machinery gliding to earth as gracefully as a feathered bird . . .

The jet had taxied to the terminal and now stood on the ramp below him. Passengers were disembarking. The luggage train drew up beside the plane. He turned and stepped to the pay phone behind him. He rang the number of an airline counter on the main floor below.

'Would you have Father Stokes paged, please? It's very important.'

'Would you repeat that?'

He repeated it, spelled his name.

'Is he on our flight?'

'I'm sure he's in the terminal.'

'I'll page him.'

'Thank you.'

He hung up the phone and started for the stairway. He came into the main waiting room with the sound of his name reverberating. There was a nice note of urgency in the pager's voice. Father Stokes assumed an expression of concern and hurried through the crowd. One or two faces connected his clerical figure with the announcement that had just been made. There were lines at the counter but he caught the eye of one of the clerks and raised his brows quizzically.

'Are you Father Stokes?'

'Yes, I am.'

The man beckoned him forward. People stood aside. 'There was a call for you, Father. Funny thing; they seem to have hung up.' He presented the phone to Stokes. The old priest held it to his ear.

'Curious,' he said. 'No one's on the line. Did it seem important?'

The man shrugged. 'I'm sorry, Father.' Stokes turned. Again the people parted to let him through. He went to the waiting room and sat down. Everyone would know now that there was a priest in the terminal. Perhaps someone would have need of him. He could easily be found, sitting there. He opened his topcoat, to make sure that his Roman collar was visible.

He should have left the phone upstairs off the hook. A simulated conversation would have made an impact. Some poor devil on the verge of suicide, desperate for discussion. Of course he would telephone Father Stokes. Just an outside chance that he might be caught at the airport. A busy man, always on assignment by his society, please God, let him be between planes. Only his voice on the phone could restrain the hand of despair. *Sed tantum dic verbo* ... A tiny plane dropped in for a landing and Father Stokes smiled at it, a proprietary smile, the smile of a man on the ready. Fear not. The plane landed safely. Stokes relaxed. He was not needed. Yet.[15]

A bit tragic and pathetic? Maybe. But this example is not so atypical, and not just of old retired priests. There is a good bit of Father Stokes in each of us. The fantasy of ourselves and of our place in reality which exists in our minds does not always fit so exactly to the real facts.

Hence we see a third type of loneliness, 'fantasy-loneliness'. Although it is evidently related to and inter-connected with the two other types of loneliness we discussed earlier, it is as unlike 'alienation-loneliness' as the young man who wrote the letter to his high school principal is unlike Father Stokes. As well, it is as unlike 'restlessness-loneliness' as Father Stokes and his problems are unlike Albert Camus, Ingmar Bergman, and the popular young girl and their problems. All of them are lonely. But their loneliness is clearly of a different genre.

(4) 'Rootlessness-loneliness'

A fourth type of loneliness can be called 'rootlessness-loneliness'. In brief, it is the type of loneliness we feel when we experience ourselves without roots, without absolutes, without anchors, adrift without a harbour in which to feel secure, without stability zones, without a meaningful grounding in a tradition, and without something which anchors us, however little, within the flow of evolution, time, and history.

There is a real loneliness in being without firm roots. It is the loneliness of ultimately having no place to lay your head. Jesus once complained that 'the son of man has no place to lay his head'.[16] One cannot help thinking that, were He walking on earth today, His complaint would be different. In all likelihood He would have a place to lay His head, but the place would be flimsily constructed, of disposable plastic (good for one year or two hundred naps), and worst of all, every time He would try to lay his head down, the place would shift!

And our world and everything in it appears to be, precisely, shifting. There is a real loneliness and pain in this. It is the loneliness and pain of being caught in a storm with no 'cleft in the rocks' to shelter us and give us some warmth and security against the cold and tempest. We can enjoy a storm, but only when we have a secure space from which we, warm and secure, can watch it and can venture in and out of it somewhat on our own conditions. If, however, we are simply caught in it, without shelter, ill-prepared and without proper dress, the storm can be a very painful experience. The storm of life is no different. If, at times at least, we can slip into a cleft in the rocks and root ourselves onto certain things which can protect us against its full brunt, we can cope with the storm. If, however, that cleft is never to be found, the storm is a cold lonely experience.

Today fewer and fewer of us are able to find that secure cleft in the rocks. Many of the things in which we used to root ourselves: family ties, religious and moral values, ideals and heroes, unshakeable truths and trusted institutions, are constantly being wrested from our grasp. For the most part, we grow up in a small nuclear family (which itself has an even chance of breaking up before we reach adulthood), with no meaningful connection with any extended family and its specific roots and traditions. We do not really know nor care whether our ancestors came from Italy, Africa, Russia, or Ireland – or whether they ate pizza, sauerkraut, or couscous! We move from place to place, eating whatever is there, forgetting our history, and letting go of many of our former religious ties and moral values. At the same time, society is debunking what remains of our moral absolutes, demythologising our former trusted institutions, and showing many of our heroes, to whom we looked for ideals and inspiration, to be morally bankrupt. Besides that, we are finding out that many of the so-called 'facts' we learned in high school and college, including mathematical facts (and what can be surer than mathematics?) are no longer valid. All our roots are constantly being cut and, as they are, we become like a boat without an anchor, set adrift, at the mercy of the winds, wanting something to clutch, but having nothing solid within our reach: neither a history nor a tradition; neither a timeless cult nor a trusted institution; neither an absolute moral imperative nor an anchor in something sacred, beyond history; indeed, not even a physical universe and a positivistic mathematics which is not relative. We are rootless! There is a loneliness which comes from being set adrift in this way.[17]

This type of loneliness is exemplified in the young person who complains that his parents have given him 'everything, except something to believe in!' One who makes such a statement is a lonely person; he has not found a 'cleft in the rocks'. We all have a need for something which is not ultimately relative, which cannot be torn down. When we do not have this, our hearts are missing something.

There is an interesting story told about the great philosopher-scientist of our century, Pierre Teilhard de Chardin. When Teilhard was just a young child of five, one day his mother was giving him a haircut. As she snipped off his locks, she tossed them into the leaping flames in the fireplace. At first the young Teilhard watched with fascination as each lock of hair burned to ashes in a matter of seconds. Then suddenly he began to cry and rushed from the room. A few days later, he began to collect pieces of iron ('because it could not be burned, but could endure fire'). Later, when he noticed that iron corroded, he discarded his iron collection and began to collect rocks instead. For him, these were ultimately indestructible. Teilhard did this when he was five years of age. Later, as an adult, his great mind would attempt to seize onto truths which were indestructible, capable of standing up to the ravages of fire and rust, whim and fashion, relativity and contingency.[18]

However, relativism works a gradual, but very real, change in our psychology and understanding of life. Today we are more used to seeing things disappear than was the young Teilhard. More typical of our age is the reaction of young Karen, the daughter of Alvin Toffler, described in *Future Shock*:

Some time ago my wife sent my daughter, then twelve, to a supermarket a few blocks from our Manhattan apartment. Our little girl had been there only once or twice before. Half an hour later she returned perplexed. 'It must have been torn down,' she said, 'I couldn't find it.' It hadn't been. New to the neighborhood, Karen had merely looked on the wrong block. But she is a child of the Age of Transience, and her immediate assumption – that the building had been razed and replaced – was a natural one for a twelve-year-old growing up in the United States at this time. Such an idea would probably never have occurred to a child faced with a similar predicament even half a century ago. The physical environment was far more durable, our links with it less transient.[19]

We are all slowly becoming like Karen, slowly learning to expect that everything will eventually be torn down. We expect things to disappear, not just old buildings, but everything! We expect our cars to rust and break down, our marriages to end in divorce, our friends to quit their jobs and move away, our priests and nuns to leave the priesthood and religious life, and people to outgrow present interests and commitments and to move on to other things. We expect our values and beliefs to become obsolete. We are beyond surprise! 'Doesn't anyone stay in one place anymore?' asks the pained artist. It would seem not.[20]

There is a loneliness caused by this, 'rootlessness-loneliness'. This loneliness is quite different from the other types of loneliness we described earlier. With this 'rootless' type, we are in lonely pain not so much because we feel alienated from others ('alienation-loneliness') or driven inwardly by perpetual restlessness ('restlessness-loneliness'), nor indeed because our fantasy of ourselves keeps us out of tune with reality ('fantasy-loneliness'), but rather because our lack of roots alienates us from the very contours of reality. We are unable to be fully friends with the real because we have not found within reality a space which is not ultimately relative or threatening, and which is therefore not liable to turn its back on us at any time. We have no cleft in the rocks from which we can venture in and out, enjoying the sunshine and taking shelter in the storm. Thus, since reality seemingly cannot give us this cleft, it is not ultimately friendly. And, if we are not fully friends with what is real, we are indeed very lonely.

(5) *'Blues-loneliness'*

The last type of loneliness can simply be called 'blues-loneliness'. As its name suggests, this is more or less 'the blues', pure and simple.

This type of loneliness is distinguishable from the other types essentially by one feature, that is, it is an ephemeral experience as opposed to one which is constant and abiding. The other types of loneliness are, for those who suffer from them, constant underlying concerns. 'Blues-loneliness', on the other hand, is something we normally experience only on a random or sporadic basis.

'Blues-loneliness' is really a form of psychological depression which people often call 'loneliness'. It is a pulse of loneliness, so to speak, which though generally short-lived, can pass through us at times, causing very intense pain, and relativising our whole life and everything which seems positive and worthwhile to us.

Often it is impossible to pinpoint with any exactitude what causes these 'blues' and what makes up the feelings contained in them. They are usually a combination of the other types of loneliness with additional depression and nostalgia. Also, a wide range of factors can trigger the 'blues' within us: anything ranging from the season of the year, to the season of our life, or the death of a loved one, or the wedding of a son or daughter, or the position of the moon, or the chemical balances within our bodies. We talk, for instance, of 'getting over a death', 'middle-age crisis', 'getting over something'; and less significantly, about 'spring fever', 'end of the semester blues', 'rainy days and Mondays', and so on. As these clichés suggest, 'blues-loneliness' can be caused by a variety of things. However, as these expressions also suggest, the 'blues' are generally an ephemeral experience, linked to some definite event, season, or happening in our lives. They can be pesky and painful at times, but for most normal people they do not constitute a major problem, except perhaps at certain times in life when specific crises such as the death of a loved one, onset of middle age, and other such happenings can render us particularly vulnerable. However, for some people, prone to depression, this type of loneliness can constitute a major threat.

Bringing the problem into theological focus

We began this chapter with a question: how can we be led out of the slavery of loneliness? By differentiating among the various types of loneliness, it becomes clearer that loneliness is not a simple phenomenon and that certain aspects of it have much more of a theological dimension than others. All types of loneliness are enslaving, but not all require as direct a theological answer. Thus, at this point, with these distinctions as a background, we can profitably take up the Christian explanation of human loneliness.

Where does Christianity speak of loneliness? Almost everywhere. As we shall see, our Scriptures and our traditions have always offered both an understanding of, and a creative resolution to, the problem of loneliness. We shall see too that the understanding offered by Christianity is an insight which goes beyond the partial and stoic answers of humanism. Furthermore, contrary to much of our conventional wisdom which sees all loneliness as bad and advises us to avoid it at all costs, our Christian understanding will challenge us to discern among the various types of loneliness; avoiding some, enduring others, and positively taking up and entering into some other types of loneliness.

Moreover, as I will try to demonstrate in the following chapters, a Christian understanding of loneliness will not only help us to understand the meaning of loneliness, but will show that some types of loneliness are really our greatest strength, our distinguishing characteristic as human beings, and something which can serve to give our lives meaning and purpose. In this sense, a Christian understanding of loneliness can be truly liberating.

As human persons caught in the throes of loneliness, we are not unlike a patient in need of psychotherapy. We yearn for help in understanding this experience, and in being able to integrate it into our lives in a meaningful way. We feel its reality and we grapple with it, but often we lack the understanding which could liberate us from its potential tyranny. My belief is that the Christian understanding of loneliness can give us this type of liberating knowledge. Christian insight can be for us a 'Moses', leading us through the 'Red Sea' to freedom, leading us beyond the condition in which we see as 'through a glass, darkly' to that promised land in which we see God and others face to face.

PART II:
TOWARDS A CHRISTIAN
UNDERSTANDING OF LONELINESS

5

THE OLD TESTAMENT ON LONELINESS

A universal story of struggle

It is hard to overestimate the importance of sharing with each other our struggles and pains. It is remarkable how much healing and courage we can derive from hearing someone else's story. Anyone who deeply and honestly shares with us the struggles of his heart, his pains and fears, helps to make us more free. This is so because their story is really, in some way, our story. It is everyone's story. When someone lays bare his heart to us we see more clearly our own heart with its pains and struggles. This is always, at least partially, a freeing experience, one which gives us greater insight into the depth and complexities of our own mysterious hearts.

Since the dawning of time there have been billions of persons born upon our earth, each of them having their own unique history and story. Countless biographies have been written, stories told, and histories recounted. Some of these are close to our own, close to our history, telling partly our story. Stories such as these offer us courage and healing, enabling us to see more clearly the meaning of our own lives.

However, few stories are as much our own biography as is the history of Israel, the story of the Old Testament.

Equally, few stories are laden with as much liberating potential and healing insight as is this story. For, looking at the Old Testament, we see not simply the story of a primitive people, but the story of the human heart; its pains and joys, its search for meaning and its search for God, its struggles with love and its struggles with loneliness.

It is a most surprising story, this book we call the Old Testament! Filled with myths, seemingly untrue stories, and historical inaccuracies, it bypasses our narrow sense of history and truth and tells us of history and truth beyond our time-conditioned and impoverished perspectives. Once properly understood it yields immense riches. It is, indeed, a most sensitively rendered story. Understood correctly, the childish-sounding myths break open into penetrating truths, the seeming historical inaccuracies begin to shed light on all history, and what on the surface looks like an ill-told story of an insignificant bedouin people tells the story of all the nations of the earth.

There may not have been a man named Adam and a woman named Eve who actually ate an apple. There may not have been a Cain who slew his brother, Abel. There may not have been a man who wrestled with an angel, nor a man named Elijah who could actually prevent the heavens from pouring forth rain. Perhaps there was never a Jonah who lived in the belly of a whale nor a town called Babel which tried to build a tower to heaven. Yet it would be wrong and impoverishing for us to think that these stories never really happened. Happen they did, to ancient men and women, in ancient towns and lands. But they are stories of the hearts of these men and women rather than video-taped documentaries on their lives. Moreover, as with all true stories of the heart, they are also the story of our hearts. As such they can provide us with much liberating insight.

And they are not just ordinary stories, sensitively rendered. They are that, but more. They are also revelation stories, revealing something about the heart of God and His understanding of our hearts. Because of this they possess a quality of timelessness, universality, insight, and healing which go beyond the power of our own stories.

In a sense, all these stories make up one story, namely that of a people struggling to see the face of God. To pierce the riddle of loneliness, the mist of unreality, and to come to full meaning and life. Because it is a story of struggle, this story can shed much light on our own struggle to break out of the slavery of loneliness and to meet others and God in intimacy and love. It can give us many healing insights into our loneliness; its cause, its meaning, and its resolution.

We turn now to look at that story to see what it can tell us about our loneliness.

Reasons for loneliness

The Old Testament does not always take up the question of loneliness explicitly, though it does at times. Hence, its analysis of and answer to the problem of human loneliness can be more profitably studied by looking at its message as a whole rather than by dwelling at length on specific texts.

What does the Old Testament see as the cause of loneliness? It sees various types of loneliness, stemming from different causes. Essentially it sees *three* causes, each of which creates a specific type of loneliness.

(1) *The loneliness which is caused by sin*[1]

The Old Testament sees sin as the prime alienator. In its view, frequently when we find ourselves lonely it is because of sin: our sin, other people's sin, or the sinful condition of the human race. Sin, since it helps destroy love and trust which can bind us together and replaces them with selfishness and distrust which help drive us apart, perhaps more than any other single force serves to alienate us from each other. Sin causes loneliness. The Old Testament sees this as happening in several ways:

First of all, sin alienates because it destroys our proper harmony with God. Loneliness results because we are now not in proper relationship with what is fully real. Moreover, this state will inevitably destroy the proper harmony and relationships we have with each other, for when we are out of tune with God, we are by that same fact out of tune with others. No one can break the first three commandments and hope to keep the other seven. In this sense, sin of all kinds makes for loneliness.

This is clearly illustrated many times in the Old Testament story. For instance, in the first eleven chapters of Genesis we see a series of sin stories: Adam and Eve, Cain and Abel, tower of Babel. Each of these shows us that when a person falls out of proper harmony with God, Yahweh, it inevitably leads to disharmony with others. The Cain and Abel story illustrates this. Very often this story is seen to be an image depicting our propensity for jealousy and its devastating effects on our interpersonal relationships. It is that, symbolically. Yet it is more. Its main purpose is theological, namely, to depict how the breakdown of harmony in our relationship to God leads always to a breakdown in harmony with each other.[2]

Israel's history as a whole further illustrates this point. Every time she is idolatrous, syncretistic, or otherwise unfaithful to her covenant with Yahweh, Israel is subject to much internal disharmony. Lack of proper harmony with God leads to a distorted view of reality. This inevitably leads to selfishness and distrust, jealousy and violence, which is the road to disharmony and loneliness.

That sin is responsible for loneliness is seen even more clearly in the Old Testament idea that sin causes direct disharmony among persons. In fact, we hardly need the

Old Testament to tell us this. We experience it every day in our lives. Nothing alienates us more from each other, driving us back into our lonely selves, than do the powers of sin. Pride and selfishness, distrust and exploitation of each other, jealousy and greediness, dishonesty and lack of openness, prejudice and unfair judgements, lack of reverence and lack of humility, these forces are like razors constantly cutting away at anything and everything which might potentially bind us together in a love which could overcome our damnable aloneness.

The Old Testament is pregnant with examples of this. One of the most penetrating of these is found right at the beginning of the Old Testament story in the account of Adam and Eve. In the book of Genesis we are told that, before their sin, 'the man and his wife were both naked, and were not ashamed'.[3] However, immediately after their sin 'the eyes of both were opened and they knew that they were naked; and they sewed fig leaves together and made themselves aprons.'[4] What is presented here is powerful symbol.

Before the sin, the man and the woman could be in each other's presence 'naked and without shame'. They could appear before each other 'unclothed', without masks, without defence mechanisms, without the need for psychological games, without façades and pretences. They could appear before each other in all their vulnerability, because, before they sinned, they trusted themselves, and consequently trusted the other. Hence, there was no need to hide things, to be protective. By sinning they lost more than their innocence. They lost their trust in themselves and, consequently, their trust in each other. They could no longer be comfortable when they were fully vulnerable to each other, and now found it necessary to protect themselves, to hide nakedness and vulnerability, to put clothes on. Sin drove both of them behind respective shelters, and effectively put a rift into their former free trusting 'naked' relationship. They now began to live in loneliness, partially hidden from each other.

We see a similar image, though perhaps even more powerful, in the story of the tower of Babel.[5] Very often this story has been taken simply as an account explaining the origin of the different languages on earth. This idea, though it makes for an imaginative and intriguing story, is far from the real intention of the sacred writer. His intent was much more theological and profound. Far from being an attempt to explain the history of languages, this story is an attempt to explain both the theological and the psychological reason for the divisions within our world, and for the alienation we experience from each other.

The author begins by depicting a previous state of harmony, like Adam and Eve's state of nakedness without shame before the fall – 'Now the whole earth had one language and few words.' Then the harmony is broken by sin: a certain town decides to 'build a tower with its top to the heavens'. However, God intervenes, and before they can finish this mammoth project, He confuses their language so that they can no longer understand each other; they begin to speak different languages and scatter to the ends of the earth.

An intriguing myth? No! This is a keenly penetrating analysis of one of the causes of human loneliness. The key to interpret the story lies in the motive for building the tower. They build it, not primarily because they want to challenge God and display their arrogance, but because they want to impress others – 'let us make a name for ourselves'. The real evil is not that the people of this town are defying the power of God, but that they are refusing to be vulnerable before others, building instead an edifice meant to impress them. Alienation results because human beings speak the same language only when they appear before each other as they really are, vulnerable, without impressively constructed towers. Vulnerability is that space within which human beings can truly meet each other and speak the same language. Sin and pride serve to destroy this space and drive us away from each other, leaving us to babble in our own language as we scatter to our respective corners of the earth.

Few images are as apt to symbolise the cause of much of our loneliness as is the story of the tower of Babel. Like the inhabitants of that town, we too are each on our own trip, attempting to construct our own impressive tower, and then wondering why nobody seems to understand the language we are speaking! We refuse to be who we are, purely and simply. Thus we alienate ourselves from each other because there is no longer any common space – a common language and a shared condition – among us. The antidote to loneliness, the path to intimacy and together-ness, lies in vulnerability and nakedness of spirit. It is not without major significance that St Luke, in describing the first Pentecost, points out that the reversal of the damage done at the tower of Babel is one of the primary reasons for the coming of the Holy Spirit.[6]

Unfortunately, we all have a propensity for building towers. We go through life refusing to be vulnerable. For example, we frequently try the Babel approach when we first meet someone. Unsure of ourselves and wanting to be accepted and liked, we quickly try to impress the new person. We parade our best wares in front of her. She is quickly made to see how bright, handsome, talented, and sensitive we really are. As well, our academic degrees and our past achievements are quickly dusted off and pre-sented. We do all this in the hope that, by seeing this beautiful tower, the other will not see us as we really are, lonely and self-conscious, unsure of ourselves as we struggle with fear and eczema. Unfortunately these attempts to overwhelm others into liking us are usually counterproductive and leave us precisely speaking another language. To our credit, usually when we notice this occurring we quickly try to pull down the tower, lower our price tag a bit, and show the other that we are rather vulnerable after all. When this happens, then friendship becomes possible because people appreciate us precisely when we are truly ourselves. Yet it is sin which, precisely, so frequently prevents us from being our true selves. We pay the price in loneliness.

(2) *The loneliness which is caused by the transitory character of all things*

'Vanity of vanity! All is vanity.' With these words, the Old Testament gives a second reason for loneliness, namely, that all with which we come into contact in this life will eventually pass away. Nothing ultimately endures. Because of this we live in constant loneliness.

We find expressions of this throughout the Old Testament story, though nowhere one which is as poignant and poetic as that provided for us by Qoheleth, the preacher.[7] He begins his fascinating work by pointing out that everything in this life is 'vanity'. Literally this means that everything is simply a vapour, an exhalation which comes into existence, but is unsubstantial and eventually vanishes. Everything is transitory. He then invites us to participate in an experiment with him. He masquerades as King Solomon ('the man who has everything') and systematically tests all the areas of life to see if he can find anything which can give him lasting fulfilment, anything which can ultimately make him unlonely. However, he finds that everything he tests – pleasure, wealth, the arts, accomplishment, hard work, power, prestige, philosophy and wisdom – is 'vanity', transitory and unsubstantial. Nothing ultimately lasts! He tests everything which could potentially give him lasting satisfaction, but at the end of each experiment he declares: 'This also is vanity and a striving after wind.'[8] He finds in this life nothing which is not passing and transitory.

From this transitory character of things comes a loneliness. Qoheleth summarises this well in the overture to his work, his poem on toil:

Vanity of vanities, says the preacher,
    vanity of vanities! All is vanity.
What does man gain by all the toil
    at which he toils under the sun?
A generation goes, and a generation comes,
    but the earth remains, forever.
The sun rises and the sun goes down,
    and hastens to the place where it rises.
The wind blows to the south,
    and goes round to the north;
round and round goes the wind,
    and on its circuits the wind returns.
All streams run to the sea,
    but the sea is not full;
to the place where the streams flow,
    there they flow again.
All things are full of weariness;
    a man cannot utter it;
the eye is not satisfied with seeing,
    nor the ear filled with hearing.
What has been is what will be,
    and what has been done is what will be done;
    and there is nothing new under the sun.
Is there a thing of which it is said,
    'See, this is new'?
It has been already,
    in the ages before us.
There is no remembrance of former things,
    nor will there be any remembrance of later things yet
    to happen among those who come after.[9]

As the story of the Old Testament clearly points out to us,
nothing ultimately lasts. This creates a certain loneliness
within each of us. We experience this type of loneliness, for
instance, when we hear of the death of a loved one; when
our children grow up and move away; when we notice our
own bodies slowly losing their youth and suppleness; or,
when we notice anything which used to be but now is no
more.

(3) *The loneliness which comes from the very nature of the human being*

The Old Testament story tells of yet another, and even more significant reason for loneliness. Very often it sees loneliness as stemming simply from the way we are built as human beings, as flowing naturally from our very nature. It singles out *three* things within our nature which are responsible for this:

(i) *Our nature is such that our desires and appetites continually outstrip our accomplishments*

The Old Testament, for the main part, understands human nature to be so fashioned that it can never come to full satisfaction because human desires always outstrip a person's actual accomplishment in this life. Our appetitive hearts are always caught in the tension of having unfulfilled desires. No amount of achievement can ever satiate us. Qoheleth puts it this way: 'All the toil of man is for his mouth, yet his appetite is not satisfied.'[10] We see this same motif present throughout the rest of the Old Testament.

Again, this hints at a reason for our loneliness, namely, our potentialities and desires are much greater than we can ever fulfil in a lifetime. Thus, we always feel somewhat unfulfilled because there are always spots inside of us which are empty. And, as we saw when we looked at the potential dangers of loneliness, it is exactly this 'emptiness' which so often propels us outward into restless and frantic activity as we try to quench a thirst in us which will not quench, and satiate a hunger which will not be satiated.

(ii) *Our nature is such that we have a certain 'timeliness' within us*

The Old Testament sees a real loneliness existing within us because of the fact that God has placed a certain 'timeliness' or 'timelessness' within our hearts.[11] This quality is seen as being something which prevents us from being fully in harmony with our surroundings.

This idea is implicit in many parts of the Old Testament, especially in the Psalms, but is spelled out explicitly by Qoheleth, the premier anthropologist of the Old Testament. Without doubt, we are familiar with his hauntingly beautiful passage on the seasons of life – 'There is a season for everything!' Unfortunately, we often stop reading this passage too soon, just before he makes his real point concerning life and human nature. He begins this passage by contrasting fourteen opposites and pointing out how God has given each its appropriate time or season. After having described this beauty and harmony of the earth ('He has made everything beautiful in its time.'), Qoheleth goes on to make a statement about human nature and its relationship to this ordered harmony, adding that God, while making everything beautiful in its own time, has put 'timeliness' into our hearts so that we are never fully in harmony with this beautiful order. The universe exists in time and is ordered according to certain laws. We, however, exist partly outside time, and thus, are partly out of tune with this order. We perpetually experience a rift between ourselves and the order of things. From this comes a certain loneliness, a certain restlessness, and a constant disquiet.

(iii) *Our nature is such that we have within ourselves an unquenchable thirst for God*

In the Old Testament we see universally present the motif that within the heart of the human person there is a burning need to meet God. This is experienced as a lonely thirst which, ultimately, will not allow itself to be frustrated, ignored, or diverted without causing much pain. Examples of this abound everywhere, especially in the Psalms:

> God, you are my God, I am seeking you.
>   my soul is thirsting for you,
> my flesh is longing for you,
>   a land parched, weary and waterless.[12]

> As a doe longs for running streams,
>   so longs my soul for you, my God.
> My soul thirsts for God,
>   the God of life;
> when shall I go to see
>   the face of God?
> I have no food but tears,
>   day and night;
> and all day long men say to me,
>   'Where is your God?'[13]

The expressions vary. Sometimes the Old Testament speaks of 'longing to see the face of God', at other times of 'yearning and pining for the courts of the Lord'.[14] Or it describes the heart as a 'parched desert' thirsting for God as a dry land thirsts for rain. Regardless of the particular expression or image used, the point is always the same: each of us has within ourselves a burning loneliness which can be quenched only by the waters which flow from the living God. No created object, or group of objects, no created person, or group of persons, be they ever so wonderful, can ever completely fill this emptiness inside us. The human heart, regardless of its time and place in history, regardless of the success or failures it meets, regardless of the amount of human affection or rejection it experiences, still yearns and pines always to see the face of God. The most important and the most deeply rooted loneliness we experience stems from this burning desire to see God.

In summary, we see that one of the main reasons of loneliness, according to the Old Testament story, stems simply from the way we are built as human beings. It appears that God has made us in such a way that there is within each of us a certain space, a thirst, a lonely emptiness which only He can fill. Consequently, as we go through this life, we are never satisfied. We are never fully satiated and fulfilled. We are always partly out of tune with the order of things and full of tension as our appetites outstrip our accomplishments. Hence, we are in perpetual disquiet as we yearn and pine for the life-giving waters that flow from the living God.

Towards a resolution of loneliness

The Old Testament not only spells out reasons for human loneliness, it also points out some concrete directions vis-à-vis a resolution of this problem. What does it see as some of the solutions to the problem? It offers *three* different types of perspectives:

(1) *Stoicism*

For a certain type of loneliness, the Old Testament does not have any answer. Like Humanistic Stoicism it sees certain types of loneliness as having no fully satisfying answer. The best we can do with some types of loneliness is to bear them as best we can. We see this type of stoic solution, for instance, in much of the book of Qoheleth. In his view, since all things are transitory, the best we can do is accept reality as it is and enjoy-it-while-it-lasts. This answer for loneliness is to fully live each moment.[15] This solution to the problem of loneliness is not to be understood in any hedonistic sense, however, as an invitation to 'eat, drink and be merry, for tomorrow we die!' But rather, what is being advocated here is honesty, a realistic facing of reality, and an acceptance and enjoyment of each moment of life for what it really is, a great (but passing) gift. This can be understood by an analogy. Imagine a cherished friend coming for a brief visit. Knowing in advance that your time together will be brief should not prevent you from enjoying the visit, but conversely, should serve to highlight the moment and make you even more aware of its importance and preciousness. A realistic acceptance of the limitations imposed by the dictates of reality can make us more fully alert to the precious gift that each moment of our life is.

The Old Testament sees this type of stoicism as the only solution to one type of loneliness, namely, that loneliness which comes to us because of the transitory nature of all things.[16]

(2) *Conversion*

Since the Old Testament sees much loneliness as stemming from sin, it is logical that it also sees conversion from sin as one of the primary paths leading out of loneliness. This idea is omnipresent in the Old Testament. Everywhere we see stressed the importance of overcoming pride, selfishness, greed, jealousy, and sin of all kinds. Return to Yahweh! Cast aside your old ways! These are perennial invitations issued to the people of the Old Testament. Conversion, the movement away from sin, the movement towards others and God, was seen as a primary means leading individuals out of loneliness towards community and fullness of life.

(3) *A community of life with God and others*

The most important way to overcome loneliness was to move more deeply into a community of life with God and one's fellow Israelites. Throughout the Old Testament we see the constant challenge and invitation: move more fully into Yahweh's community of love and life, live more fully as a partner in the covenant.

The Israelite people of the Old Testament believed that, from the time of Abraham onwards, Yahweh had chosen them to be in a special relationship of love with Him; that He had made a covenant with them, binding Himself to be in a community of life with them. This was the ultimate solution for every problem, including loneliness. This community of life, if properly lived, was seen as being capable of providing that extra dimension which could eventually still and fulfil the loneliness in each person's heart. For them, whether one lived or died, whether one was happy or sad, and whether one was lonely or fulfilled depended mainly upon how vital their relationship was to that community of life, the covenant. For the Old Testament peoples, the final and only solution to the problem of loneliness lay in being vitally linked with this community of life. Hence, the path leading out of loneliness was seen to lie in *prayer* (which moved one into a deeper community of life with God) and in *following the law and practising charity* (which moved one into a deeper community of life with others). Within this community of life, loneliness would eventually disappear.

It is interesting to notice that, for the most part, the Old Testament peoples had no clear idea as to how this community of life would fully take their loneliness away. They did not know what the final fulfilment would consist in. They simply had faith in Yahweh, believing that somehow He would accomplish this – providing that they trusted Him enough to give Him the space He needed to be God and that they 'hung in there' long enough to allow Him to accomplish His plans.[17]

Later on the classical prophets would add an extra dimension to this. They believed that things at present were inadequate and incomplete, painful and lonely. However, they continually invited the people to move more deeply into community of life with each other and with Yahweh, believing that at a certain point Yahweh would do a radically new saving act (one as powerful as the original act of creation). He, Yahweh, would declare a new age and pour out his Spirit upon the whole earth. This would make creation very different than it was at present. The prophets had no clear vision of what specifically Yahweh would do, what would happen, or what the end result would look like. They only knew that if one remained within Yahweh's community of life, sooner or later He would act. He would send some messiah, an anointed one, a saviour, a son of man. With Him would come the outpouring of His Spirit, the *Ruah Yahweh*. And when this happened, creation would be turned delightfully upside down. Wolves would play with lambs; lions with baby calves. Little children would play with poisonous snakes, young and old alike would see visions, and Yahweh, Himself, would come and wipe away all tears and loneliness forever.[18]

6

THE NEW TESTAMENT ON LONELINESS

Christ as the definitive answer

The Old Testament gives us some invaluable perspectives on loneliness, throwing much light on both its cause and its resolution. Yet, when the story finishes, we are left with more of a promise than a fully satisfying answer. Israel's story sets down the direction within which an answer lies, but it ends just before that direction is completely spelled out. Thus, the Old Testament story leaves us with a heart that is only partially placated; some of the question remains unanswered.

What will take our loneliness fully away? Jesus comes as the full definitive answer to that question. He comes as the living water, able to fully placate and put to rest the lonely questions and yearnings within our hearts. In His person and in His message, He addresses Himself directly to the problem of loneliness. He comes preaching a 'kingdom', a 'reign of God', and a 'new life' which is 'not food and drink', but one composed of 'righteousness and peace and joy in the Holy Spirit'.[1] He presents Himself as ushering in this kingdom which, as foretold by the Old Testament prophets, would turn reality delightfully upside down; stripping the lonely pain of unconsummated love from our hearts, and putting an end to pain and suffering forever.

Unfortunately, too often when we look at the message that Christ preached, at His words about establishing a kingdom, we tend to spiritualise them and abstract them from the ordinary bread-and-butter problems of life. We consider it too banal to connect Jesus' talk about a king-dom with such an unspiritual thing as loneliness. Conse-quently we too seldom connect Jesus' person and His message to any meaningful areas within our lives, es-pecially the 'unchurchy' ones such as loneliness. Yet so much of His message speaks precisely (and undisguisedly) about loneliness, the burning thirsts within our hearts. Ironically, perhaps, one of the clearer expressions of the significance of Jesus' message vis-à-vis loneliness comes from a non-Christian, Thomas Wolfe. In his essay, 'God's Lonely Man', he speaks about how much Jesus' message addresses itself to this issue:

> The central purpose of Christ's life, therefore, is to destroy the life of loneliness and to establish here on earth the life of love. The evidence to support this is clear and overwhelming . . .

> (Christ's message) tells men that they shall not live and die in loneliness, that their sorrow will not go unassuaged, their prayers unheard, their hunger and thirst unfed, their love unrequited: but that, through love, they shall destroy the walls of loneliness forever; and even if the evil and unright-eous of this earth shall grind them down into the dust, yet if they bear all things meekly and with love, they will enter into a fellowship of joy, a brotherhood of love, such as no men on earth ever knew before.

> Such was the final intention of Christ's life, the purpose of His teaching. And its import was that the life of loneliness could be destroyed forever by the life of love. Or such, at least, has been the meaning which I read into His life. For in these recent years when I have lived alone so much, and know loneliness so well, I have gone back many times and read the story of this man's words and life to see if I could find in them a meaning for myself, a way of life that would be better than the one I had. I read what He had said, not in a mood of piety or holiness, not from a sense of sin, a feeling of contrition, or because His promise of heavenly reward meant very much to me. I tried to read His bare words nakedly and simply, as it seems to me He must have uttered them, and as I have read

the words of other men – of Homer, Donne, and Whitman, and the writer of Ecclesiastes – and if the meaning I have put upon His words seems foolish or extravagant, childishly simple or banal, mine alone or not different from what ten million other men have thought, I have only set it down here as I saw it, felt it, found it for myself, and have tried to add, subtract, or alter nothing.[2]

When we look at Jesus' message and try to 'add, subtract, or alter nothing', we too see that much of His message relates itself to loneliness. In fact we see in Jesus' message the definitive analysis of human loneliness, both in terms of its causes and the direction we must take in order to come to a creative resolution of this problem.

What defining perspectives does Jesus give?

Reasons for loneliness

The Old Testament, in its analysis of human loneliness, has already marked out the essential direction within which an understanding of this problem can take place. The New Testament simply deepens and clarifies these perspectives to the point where they become definitive. Also, as is the case with the Old Testament, the New Testament's perspectives on loneliness are best gleaned from looking at its message as a whole rather than by looking for a few explicit texts upon which to attempt to build a theology.

The New Testament sees human loneliness as essentially caused by *two* factors:

(1) *The loneliness of sin*

As in the Old Testament, sin is seen as a prime alienator. Sin causes us to lose harmony with God and each other. Because of sin, we live in loneliness and isolation, deprived of much of the intimacy, empathy, and friendship which could lessen some of our loneliness.

In its discussion on sin as causing loneliness, the New Testament reveals some interesting dimensions of this problem. It sees the loneliness which results from sin as being, not just metaphorically, but actually, the experience of hell. Jean-Paul Sartre, the French philosopher, once remarked that 'hell is the other'. The New Testament reverses this. Hell is the experience of loneliness which results because of our pride, selfishness, and sin.

This idea is present implicitly many times in the New Testament but is given explicit expression by St Paul in his Epistle to the Romans.[3] Paul does not understand God's wrath, the punishment of hell, as consisting in some extrinsic punishment. For him it is never a question of God positively punishing persons because they have sinned ('laying on' punishment, so to speak). Rather the punishment flows naturally and intrinsically from the sin itself. An analogy will help clarify this. If a person drinks too much alcohol the natural consequence is a painful headache. However, this hangover is not something which God, nor anyone else, needs to impose in order to let the person know that he had done something wrong. Hangovers are not willed by anyone! They simply flow intrinsically from overdrinking. The punishment comes from the crime, not from some outside judge and vindicator.

It is in this same fashion that the New Testament views hell as a natural consequence of sin. And, in this case, hell is loneliness. When we sin we cut ourselves off from others and retreat inside ourselves, with only our own pride and selfishness for companions. This is hell. Like a hangover, though infinitely worse, hell is not some extrinsic punishment imposed upon us by a God who is eager to safeguard His justice and to let us know we have sinned. Rather hell is simply the burning painful thirst of culpable alienation, neither willed by God nor any other outside judge, which results intrinsically from sin, from making ourselves our own God and refusing to move out towards others with openness and altruism. Sin is a tremendously alienating force at every level of existence.

(2) *The loneliness of being a pilgrim on earth*

The Old Testament, as we saw, affirms that there is a certain loneliness which exists, not because of sin or any other culpable factor, but because the human heart, by nature, is insatiable, filled with timelessness, and thirsting constantly for the infinite riches of God. The New Testament reveals this motif further, giving it a more definitive expression by setting it into a wider salvation history and anthropological framework.

The New Testament affirms that we are lonely because we are pilgrims on earth.[4] As we journey through this life, looking to love and live meaningfully, we are constantly unable to find full satisfaction and fulfilment. Why? Because like a traveller or a pilgrim in a foreign country we are never really at home. We might even enjoy the journey, but nowhere do we find a permanent resting place which is fully our own and which gives us complete satisfaction. Hence, we go through life always a little lonely, a little restless, a little dissatisfied, unable to fully settle into any final state of rest or comfort. In the words of the author of the Epistle to the Hebrews, 'Here we have no lasting city, but we seek the city which is to come.'[5] This makes for a certain loneliness since our pilgrim status urges us on and makes us constantly restless as we look for an eternal city.

A famous story, often retold, illustrates what is implied in being a pilgrim on earth. In the last century, a tourist from America paid a visit to the renowned Polish rabbi Hofetz Chaim. The tourist was astonished to see that the rabbi's home was only a simple room filled with books, plus a table and a bench.

'Rabbi,' asked the tourist, 'where is your furniture?'

'Where is yours?' replied Hofetz Chaim.

'Mine?' asked the puzzled American. 'But I'm only a visitor here. I am only passing through.'

'So am I,' said the rabbi.

We are all only passing through!

That we are pilgrims on earth is so evident and omnipresent in the New Testament that it would be superfluous to attempt to substantiate this claim by making reference to a number of specific texts and sayings of Jesus. His whole message presupposes this and is unintelligible without this understanding as part of its background. Christ presupposes that the human heart cannot come to full satisfaction on its own, in its present condition in this world. He sees us as dwelling here but for a short time. Thus, Jesus, and the rest of the New Testament following Him, constantly exhorts us to live as if this life is not all there is; to live in vigilance, to not take the pleasures of this life too seriously, to have a perspective which opens us beyond the purely intramundane, and to be willing to sacrifice much, perhaps even our life itself, for a new life and kingdom which lies partly beyond this world.

However, a note of caution is important here. The message of Jesus and the New Testament is not totally 'next-worldly'. Christ did not come to refocus our attention entirely beyond the boundaries of this life, nor to give us an 'opium' that would enable us to either ignore or disdain the here-and-now, seeing it simply as a 'vale of tears' to be endured as we wait for a more blessed state. His promise of a kingdom (Synoptics) and a new life (John) has a dimension which begins already now, in this world.[6] Conversely, nowhere is the promise of a kingdom of love and new life, a state of fully consummated and ecstatic togetherness, ever presented as being completely identifiable with any condition or state in this life, however idyllic. Neither is the kingdom ever seen as being simply the natural outgrowth of a practice of virtue and goodness; rather it is always seen as something which Christ's coming inaugurates, which then is partly realised in this life, but which will only eventually be brought to consummation by a further act of God. For most of us, unless the world ends before we die, full satisfaction and the complete removal of loneliness must wait until after we die. Here in this life, we live always in partial loneliness; incomplete and thirsty, restless and in pain, as we say the Lord's Prayer and wait in hope for the kingdom to fully come.

Jesus and the New Testament base this understanding of our pilgrim condition on two interconnected things: *their understanding of anthropology and their understanding of the time-framework within which salvation history takes place.*

(i) *Jesus' understanding of the human heart*

Jesus and the New Testament in general understand the human being to be so fashioned that there is within him/her a capacity to receive and respond to the very life of God, the Trinitarian life. Hence Jesus believes and His whole message presupposes that the human heart has infinite capacities for life and love. He calls each of us to live within the very life of the Godhead, to be at an eternal banquet with God and all others who are sincere, and to be part of the formation of His very body. This presupposes some pretty astounding capabilities on our part. And, given the capacity for the infinite, it is not surprising that anything we can attain, save that, is painfully inadequate.

We are called to relate to an Infinite Love, to live within the very life of God, and eventually to be in an ecstatic all-embracing togetherness with all others of good will and even with the material universe. Is it so surprising then, that as we go through life, with all its riddles, frustrations, and partial answers, that we are constantly lonely?

(ii) *Jesus' understanding of the time-framework of salvation history*

In order to understand what it means to be a pilgrim on this earth, and that a certain loneliness flows from this reality, it is critical and necessary to situate ourselves within the framework of salvation history.

All of us have a certain grasp of where we are situated within world history, and, to a lesser extent, where we stand in terms of cosmic history, the history of our universe. We know that we live in the twentieth century, a few billion years after the formation of our planet, earth; a few million years after the advent of life; a few hundred thousand years after the moment of hominisation; a few thousand years after the dawning of civilisation and the birth of Christ (A.D.); and a few years after the two world wars and the great depression of our own century. According to some anthropologists we are in the 800th lifetime of man.[7]

But in what age or lifetime are we in God's eyes? What is our status, our situation, our position within the widest historical framework of all, the history of salvation? This is indeed a significant question, one which has immense consequences for our self-understanding and, ultimately, for our understanding of loneliness.

Jesus defines for us our place within the time-framework of salvation history. For Him, history as seen through God's eyes has definite phases. The first phase began with the original creation. God, through His Spirit and His word, brought the heavens and the earth into existence. After a time ('six days') the human race appeared within this creation. Almost immediately there was, because of sin and human inadequacy, a universal need for divine help in order to bring the human race to fulfilment. Left to themselves, the human species and each member of that species, would have been doomed to be ultimately frustrated. Therefore God begins to act in order to bring about this fulfilment. Through Israel, He begins to speak explicitly to the human race, revealing some of Himself and His plan. He reveals that eventually He will enact a new phase of history, an entirely new age, which will be the final age of history. He promises that, in this new age, He will speak His full and definitive word, pour out His Spirit, and draw all people of good will into His very own life. This new age would be very different from the previous one. In it, history would be turned delightfully upside down, wolves would lie down with lambs, lions with calves, and all sincere persons would be drawn into a radical community of life with each other and with God Himself.

Christ understands this final age, the final *eschaton*, as breaking into history with His coming, especially with His resurrection from the dead. With that, the old age is over; something radically new is here. We are now in the final age that was promised by God in the Old Testament. History is upside down.

However, Christ saw this new age, itself, as having two phases:[8] *an interim (partially realised) phase and a fully consummated phase*. It is critical to distinguish between the two phases of history within this final age.

With Christ begins a radically new phase of history, almost as radical as that begun at the original creation. However, this new age, in which lamb and wolf will lie down together, and in which we will be drawn into ecstatic union with God and each other, though already here, is not yet fully realised. It still needs to be brought to full completion. This will happen only when Christ returns in glory at the end of time. In the meantime, the time in-between Christ's resurrection and His return, we live in a time of tension between the *already* and the *not yet*. We are *already* redeemed, *already* living in the Spirit, *already* raised from the dead, and *already* in radical community of life with God and each other.[9] The Kingdom of God is *already* here. However it is *not yet* here in all its fullness. We are still *awaiting* full redemption, *awaiting* complete life in the Spirit, *awaiting* full resurrection, and *awaiting* full ecstatic community with God and each other. We are still waiting for the wolf and the lamb, the lion and the calf, the cow and the bear, and the young child and the snake to fully 'get it together'! We are still waiting for a full resolution to our loneliness.

We live in the final eschatological age, but in an interim phase of that period. Moreover, the phase in which we live

is not characterised by complete fulfilment, but rather by
tension. The Old Testament sage says: 'There is a time for
everything!' Our own time in salvation history is a time of
partial fulfilment, a time of *incompleteness*, a time of
waiting, a time of *working*, a time of *pilgrimage* and
partial loneliness.[10] We actually possess the new life. But
the possession of it is in faith, in hope, and in charity. Here
we live in tension and incompleteness; having something,
but not fully; living in hope, but having to hope against
hope; living in faith, but having to gamble real life on
seeming unreality; living in charity, but having to love
and work unselfishly in the face of incompleteness and
loneliness.

We are pilgrims on earth. We are living in the final age
of history, but are destined to be partly lonely until Jesus
returns. Our loneliness will only be fully overcome then,
when He returns, rips aside the veil of faith, makes the
object of our hope fully visible, blows the trumpet to
announce that all this waiting has been worthwhile, that
the love banquet is about to begin in all its fullness, and
that there are going to be some incredibly delightful
surprises long before the meal gets well under way.[11]

Towards a resolution: definitive directions

The New Testament's solution to the problem of human
loneliness is already implicit in its analysis of its causes. If
the causes of loneliness are sin and our pilgrim status on
earth, then correspondingly, the solution to human loneliness must lie in the direction of *conversion* and in *an
ever-deepening growth into the kingdom that Jesus pro-
claimed*. Both of these elements are already contained in
Jesus' opening lines in Mark's gospel: 'The time is fulfilled, the kingdom of God is at hand; repent, and believe in
the gospel.'[12] With these words, Jesus invites us to resolve
our loneliness by moving in a certain direction: *Away from
sin and towards the gospel*.[13]

(i) *Away from sin*

'Sin breeds sin', are the words of an old adage. Unfortunately it also breeds much loneliness. It is the prime alienator, constantly severing the bonds of friendship and love with each other. Hence, as is the case for the Old Testament, the first step towards moving out of loneliness is to convert, to turn our life around, away from pride and selfishness, jealousy and distrust, pettiness and hardheartedness, and all the many other things which keep us locked in our own lonely shells.

There is only one way to break out of these shells, and that is the road of conversion. Let the one who would be unlonely take Jesus' challenge seriously: begin to live the Sermon on the Mount;[14] begin to see the face of God in the needs of others;[15] begin to live as one in waiting;[16] begin to become part of Christ incarnate;[17] begin to draw life from the sacramental Christ;[18] and begin to follow Jesus to Jerusalem![19]

(ii) *Towards the Gospel*

However, a simple movement away from sin, without an accompanying movement towards something else, is not enough. We find ourselves on this earth as pilgrims, possessive of some astoundingly deep capacities, sensitivities, and cravings. We go through life hungering and thirsting for both the infinite and the finite. Our hearts desire not just the infinite, that which is beyond the persons and things we know, but also the finite, the persons and the things we do know. We want both.

But what can ever quench such a loneliness? Union, communion, consummation. Our loneliness will be fully satisfied by our coming together in a radical union with God, others, and the very elements of the cosmos; a union in which we will not be swallowed up, as a drop in the ocean, but in which we will each still have our own identity (indeed a heightened individuality), despite the all-consuming unity.[20] But is this possible?

Christ answers that, not only is it possible, but it is the very end to which we are called, and for which we are made. We are called to turn away from sin and to turn precisely towards *that*: a *kingdom* of togetherness, a *new life* of union with God and others, a life of *grace*. At the very centre of Christ's person and message lies the promise to draw all His children into a community of life and love, a community of ecstatic togetherness which will take away all loneliness forever. For Christ, this is the definitive answer to human loneliness. We are built for this community of life. Thus, everything else will be only partially fulfilling. All attempts to resolve our loneliness outside of this community of life are doomed, at some point, to be frustrating. There is, indeed, just the one way![21]

Even this community of life, however, does not resolve all our loneliness immediately. This community is the kingdom of God which Christ came to bring. That kingdom, as we saw, has two phases to it: an already-realised-phase, which began with Christ's entry into the world, and a fully-consummated-phase, which will occur only when Christ returns at the end of time. Until that time, or until the time of our death, we will always be partially lonely as we wait for the full kingdom. However even here, our degree of loneliness will be largely contingent upon our degree of integration into this community of life, the community of all sincere persons.

How do we enter this community of life, this kingdom, the realm of grace? Jesus' answer is clear. Entry into the kingdom, the community of life, is not contingent upon some mysterious initiation, nor upon some chance meeting of the right guru. Nor does one enter this kingdom sheerly through the force of a brilliant intelligence, a noble birth, or through pure chance or luck. Entrance into this kingdom is not restricted to chance and to a few élite, privileged, brilliant, or lucky persons. *The kingdom is open to all!*[22] What Christ does require for entry is purity of heart, an openness to God and to others.[23] There are no hidden secrets, accessible only to the élite; in fact, the élite often have to turn to little children to get their information on this question. Little children seem to understand how to enter; the poor get in without paying; the outcasts are admitted and get the best seats; and many very *ordinary* persons are entering without even knowing theology! It is a very open system that Christ is running: 'The Spirit and the Bride say, "Come". And let him who hears say, "Come". And let him who is thirsty come, let him who desires take the water of life without price.'[24]

Summary – 'as through a glass, darkly'

St Paul aptly summarises the New Testament's view on loneliness by using a very powerful metaphor. In 1 Corinthians 13, he writes:

> For now we see in a mirror dimly (as through a glass, darkly), but then face to face. Now I know in part; then I shall understand fully, even as I have been fully understood.[25]

What Paul is doing here is contrasting how we live and love *now*, as opposed to how we will live and love *when God's kingdom is fully established*. Now, before our death, we live and love as through a 'glass, darkly'. Our life is lived within a certain mist of unreality, within a certain fantasy, within a certain loneliness. We never see God, others, or reality as they really are ('face to face'), but see only certain reflections of them, as one sees an image in a mirror. Hence we are always partially separated from everything else, living behind a veil and having to sort through a riddle in order to try to meet fully God and others. Only after our death will this veil be fully stripped away and then we will encounter God and others face to face. Only then will we be entirely unlonely.

In using this image, Paul is drawing upon an Old Testament metaphor, namely, *the face of God* motif. In the

Old Testament, God is always understood to be veiled, partially hidden. No one ever sees Him directly. There is present the idea that nobody can look upon the face of God and live.[26]

As the Old Testament develops so too does this motif of *the face of God*. It begins, at a certain point, to refer not just to the veil of faith which separates us from God, but also to the fact that, as persons, we live our lives within a certain riddle, behind a veil which separates us partly from all that is real, and keeps us lonely. Eventually the Old Testament people begin to express all the longings within their hearts with this plea: 'Lord, show us your face!' In effect, they are really saying: 'Lord, remove the riddle, the veil, the mirror of unreality, show us Yourself and each other! Take our loneliness away!'[27]

The Old Testament ends with the question: 'Where can we see the face of God?' 'Who can see God face to face?' But this question is not primarily a theological one, namely, 'What does God look like?' Or even, 'Who has the best chance of going to heaven?' Nor is it simply an appeal for faith: 'Lord, help my unbelief!' No, it is precisely an existential question, coming from the pain of a lonely heart that is asking God how the loneliness we live in, the mist of unreality which separates us from Him and others, can be pierced. How can we become fully unlonely?

Jesus, in His most famous sermon ever, answers that question: 'Blessed are the pure of heart, for they shall see God.'[28] These words by Jesus must be understood with that background in mind. His Jewish listeners would have made the connection, that is, we cut through the riddle of life, we pierce the mist of loneliness and encounter God and others face to face, to the extent that we attain purity of heart. The whole Christian life (and also that which has classically been called 'the Spiritual life') is nothing other than this, namely, an attempt to strip aside the veils and mirrors, riddles and walls, barriers and shadows, fears and fantasies, façades and mists, and the selfishness and unreality which separate us from God and each other. The

Christian life is an attempt to pierce the mist of unreality and encounter God and others face to face. To the extent that this happens in our lives, we enter the kingdom of God, the community of life, which will wipe away all our tears and take our loneliness fully away. To the extent that this happens in our lives we go to heaven.

I would like to illustrate this whole idea in a more existential way by referring to two films by Ingmar Bergman: *Through a Glass Darkly* and *Face to Face*. As is obvious from the titles, there is a clear, though metaphorical, reference to what St Paul speaks about in 1 Corinthians 13.

The film *Through a Glass Darkly*[29] illustrates existentially what is involved in living 'as through a glass, darkly.' In its own way, this film, like the Old Testament Psalmist, pleads: 'Lord, let me see your face!' The story is centred on the riddle of life. Bergman's four characters – Karin, Martin, David, and Minus – are bound together in a family, and are desperately trying to reach and love each other, but are not succeeding too well. Each is trapped in his or her own world, inside his/her lonely self behind some barrier which separates him/her from the other and from the contours of life in general. Karin, presented as having the most serious problem, is suffering from an incurable mental illness which causes her to lose contact with reality and become ensnared in a nightmare of fears, dreams and illusions. Her pains and struggles to reach others and to stay in contact with reality are paradigmatic of every person's struggle to do just that. Her mental illness symbolises what St Paul means when he says that now we see God and others as 'through a glass, darkly'. We are all separated, in some way, from reality, struggling to stay in contact.

A victim of her illness, Karin lives in frustration and loneliness, unable, except for an occasional moment here and there, to break through and really meet others and share life with them. She is lucid enough to know what is happening and that serves to make her pain all the more tragic and unbearable. As well, her lucidity causes her to be filled with feelings of panic and desperation. The other characters, too, are trying to sort through their own riddles. Everyone is, ultimately, seeing as 'through a glass, darkly'.

More recently, Bergman has released a film called *Face to Face*.[30] This movie takes up the same theme as *Through a Glass Darkly* but develops it further. The story portrays the suicide attempt of a lady psychiatrist, Jenny, a very successful, respected, loved, and well-adjusted person. Yet at a certain point, she decides to attempt suicide. She overdoses with sleeping pills. There follows a long sequence in which the film takes up her dream as she is seemingly sleeping her way to death. However, at this point, Bergman deliberately blurs the distinction between her fantasy and reality so that we no longer know whether Jenny is asleep or awake. We simply share in her struggle as she tries to sort her way through the mist which holds her back from full consciousness. During this sequence, many poignant metaphors are depicted: her struggle to fight her way to full consciousness is presented as a parable for all of life. We see poor Jenny constantly caught in a fog, locked behind closed doors which seem to promise life and contact with others, but which will not open for her; calling out to people who are close by, but who cannot seem to hear her; and struggling to fight her way through a confusing mist, to reality, to meet someone, anyone!

A friend discovers her before she dies and takes her to a hospital. The latter part of the movie is centred on her dialogue with the male doctor who is trying to help her recover. At one point, in the recovery room she asks him:

'What do you want from life? What would have to happen to make it meaningful?'

He replies, 'Just once I would like something to be real!'

'Real? What do you mean?' Jenny replies.

He answers, 'Just once I would like to reach through to someone and see someone and touch someone, and know that that other person is just as real as I am. Just once I would like to cut through all the veils and barriers, mirrors and fantasies, shadows and unrealities which separate us from each other and feel something as real as I am. Just once I would like to see face to face. Then life would be meaningful.'[31]

Is it not this which would also make each of our own lives meaningful? Is this not what St Paul is describing in 1 Corinthians 13? Is this not what the kingdom of God is really all about? Has not Christ called us precisely to break through the mirrors and riddles, the shadows and fantasies, the façades and unrealities which separate us from each other and from God so that we can all meet face to face? Has not Christ called us to pierce the dim reflection? Heaven, and a full answer to our loneliness, lies in doing just that.[32]

SOME CHRISTIAN THEOLOGIANS ON LONELINESS

The value of tradition

'There are only two or three human stories, and they go on repeating themselves as fiercely as if they had never happened.'[1] These words sum up the value of history and tradition.

Every generation of humans must struggle with certain problems which arise at the very centre of its experience. In struggling with these problems, each generation is tempted to see itself as unique, as so different from past generations as to be unable to be helped by former insights and perspectives. It is true that each generation is unique and fraught with its own novel complexities. However, each generation is also very much part of a universal human story; since the dawn of consciousness, the human heart has had to struggle with essentially the same questions. Always the questions have been of life and death, meaning and despair, love and loneliness. There have been only a few great questions, just as there have been only a few great stories.

Throughout history therefore we see many minds like our own, and at times, minds greater than our own, struggling with *our* problems. Meeting these minds can be a healing and enlightening experience since very often the perspectives they have produced shed light on our own struggle for liberating insight and catharsis. If we forget our history, we are condemned to relive it. If we refuse to look to history and tradition for insight, we are condemned to struggle alone, without the aid of much that can be helpful to us. Our story has been told before. Hearing it can be therapeutic for us in our own struggle to come to inner freedom and understanding.

As Christians today we are richly blessed since we stand within a tradition which draws upon the wealth of nearly four thousand years of struggle and insight. We have already seen how both the Old and New Testaments view loneliness. Now it remains for us to ask the question: how has human loneliness been viewed throughout nearly two thousand years of post-biblical tradition? How did the fathers of the church and the later theologians answer this question?

The Christian tradition has always addressed itself to this question, either explicitly or implicitly. As we shall see, it has many valuable insights to share. However, it would be too mammoth a task to attempt to give a complete overview of the Christian tradition on loneliness. Instead what will be offered is the view of four theologians, each of whom represents a different age within church history, and who together span some sixteen hundred years of Christian tradition. Each, in his own way, tells our story. Each offers some valuable perspectives towards understanding loneliness. Together they offer a representative Christian viewpoint.

Hence we look to *Augustine* (AD 354–430), *Thomas Aquinas* (AD 1225–1274), *John of the Cross* (AD 1542–1591), and *Karl Rahner* (1904–1984) to see what they can tell us about our story, especially as it relates to our struggle to understand and free ourselves from the potential tyranny of our loneliness.

Augustine (AD 354–430)

'You arouse him to take joy in praising you, for you have made us for yourself, and our heart is restless until it rests in you.'[2] With these words, Augustine sums up an entire anthropology and an explanation for human loneliness as well.

These words however become fully intelligible only when they are placed within Augustine's anthropology in general. How did Augustine understand the human person? Why are our hearts restless until they rest in God?

For Augustine, the human person is someone God creates because of His goodness and love. God's love is so great that it cannot contain itself. It is 'effervescent', ever bubbling up and bursting forth to create beings with which to share itself. Hence, the human person is nothing other than something which God's love has created with which to share Himself. As humans, then, we are born to participate in the richness of God's very life. Accordingly, since this is our purpose, the only thing which can give us full happiness and completion is, precisely, God's life, full union with God.

However, while we are on earth, separated from full union with God by our creatureliness and by sin, we live a mixed existence, partly living within the city of God and partly living within the city of man. This leaves us incomplete and thirsty, restless and lonely, longing always to bring this pilgrimage to an end, to return to God and our true homeland.

In such a perspective *our loneliness is really nothing other than our thirst and restlessness to return to God*, to full completion within that richness which is divine life. While we are living on this earth, we are pilgrims, aliens from our true homeland. We live therefore in pain and disquiet, in restlessness and anticipation, as we wait for the journey to end.[3]

For Augustine, loneliness is both a very good and a very natural thing. It is God's way of drawing us towards the life for which we were made. God wants us to live His life, and so He placed within us a strong erotic thirst, a loneliness, which forces us to constantly yearn for Him, and to be frustrated and not content when we are outside His life.

Understanding this properly can be a very liberating

insight because, since the dawn of human consciousness, people have ever been at a loss to explain themselves. We never seem to be able to figure out why so frequently when we want to relax, we cannot; why so frequently when we want to work, we do not; and why so frequently when we want to be disciplined, we are not. We are without explanation as to why we are always so restless and unable to sit still. We are constantly surprised (not to mention disappointed) with ourselves. The philosopher, Blaise Pascal, once remarked, 'The sole cause of man's unhappiness is that he does not know how to stay quietly in his room.'[4] How true! And yet how natural! For Augustine, this is not a great mystery or an astounding anomaly. We cannot stay quietly in our room precisely because God did not build us to stay quietly in a room. We are built to wander, to be restless and lonely. Accordingly we should not be so surprised if we find ourselves incurably in that condition.

Augustine based this anthropology and understanding of loneliness, not just on his Christian faith and his Neo-platonic background,[5] but especially on his own life's experience. Most of us are familiar with his life and his search for meaning, a search which led him through philosophy, hedonism, and at times even through perversion.[6] Reading through his *Confessions*, one can see the tremendous struggle – intellectual, emotional, and moral – that he underwent before he finally came to this understanding of the human heart and human loneliness. When he makes his famous statement (perhaps the most quoted line in all of his writings) 'you have made us for yourself, and our heart is restless until it rests in you,' he is not just stating a theological conclusion that he has come to as a result of some exegetical and systematic research. He is telling the story of his life, the story of our life, and the story of every person who has ever searched and cried in loneliness, wandered and wondered in restlessness, and lived in pain while seeing life as through a glass, darkly.

Thomas Aquinas (AD 1225–1274)

The medieval theologian, Thomas Aquinas, also offers some valuable perspectives vis-à-vis the question of human loneliness. Like Augustine before him, he bases his explanation of loneliness on an understanding of human nature and how he sees it as relating to God. For him, we are lonely because God built us that way. However, while being similar to Augustine on this point, he develops Augustine's understanding of loneliness on *three* significant points:[7]

(1) *Loneliness is not just a thirst for God, but a thirst for other persons and the world as well*

For Augustine, we are lonely because our hearts are restless until they attain God. Thomas goes further and adds an important nuance to this explanation.[8] Complete rest for our lonely hearts will, according to him, come only when we are in full union with God, and with each other and the whole of reality. Thus, Thomas would re-cast slightly the Augustinian dictum, making it read: 'You have made us for yourself, and our heart is restless until it rests in you . . . *and others, and the whole world.*'

(2) *Loneliness is what makes us dynamic beings*

According to Thomas, the human person is a creature whom God has created for a very definite purpose and end. What is that purpose? From explicit Christian revelation we see that we are made for beatific vision, heaven, for union with God and others in a kingdom of love. As well, from philosophy we see that we are made to attain perfect Being, perfect Love, and perfect Truth. As Scholastic philosophers classically put it: the adequate object of our intellect and will (that which can give us total meaning and satisfaction) is union in knowledge and love with all of Being.[9]

As persons, we are called to this end both by God's explicit word (scripture) and by the erotic urgings right within our own psychological and physical structure. Built for union, called and drawn towards it in mind and body, it follows logically that we must be capable of attaining it. And, given the fact that we are capable of infinite love and knowledge, it follows that we can never be completely fulfilled, completely happy, or completely at rest until we have attained that end. Lesser ends will simply not satisfy us. We are doomed to critique every experience we have in the light of our ultimate potential. That is why we are always lonely.

Put in summary fashion, Thomas is saying this: we are built for the infinite, to be in perfect intercommunity with God and others. We hunger for this, long for it, and constantly and thirstily reach out for it. But, when we do reach out, we can meet and touch only particular persons and objects. These can fulfil us to a point, but never completely. Our nature is built for more and it demands more. Accordingly we go through life always somewhat lonely and dissatisfied, restless and unfulfilled, as we perpetually reach out and seek that radical unity with God and others for which we were made.

In such a perspective, loneliness becomes a good thing, a valuable and necessary force in our lives. It is the force which drives us to keep searching, to keep reaching, to not give up. It is the force which keeps us dissatisfied with pseudo and partial solutions, with hedonistic and short term answers. It is the force which keeps us dynamic, making us restless and dissatisfied when we are stagnant, and making us constant critics of our experience in the light of the very reason for which we were made.

(3) *Loneliness, if listened to, tells us of God's purpose for us*

In Thomas' view, our loneliness is a good force not only in that it keeps us dynamic, but also because it keeps us constantly focused on the end for which God made us. He explains this as follows: we are made to be in ecstatic union with God and others. This is our purpose. How do we know that purpose? We come to know it, not just through explicit Christian revelation, but simply by listening to and following the inner dictates and urges of our own being. Through loneliness, God has written His plan for us right into the very structures of our heart, mind, and body. Loneliness is His imprint in us, constantly telling us where we should be going.

An analogy can be used to explain Thomas' idea here: after a clockmaker builds a watch he does not need to tell it explicitly that its task is to keep time. Rather he builds it in such a way that, following its own natural dictates, rhythms, and structures, it will naturally keep time. Its own internal mechanisms, its wound-up springs, cause a corresponding tension which naturally causes its hands to move . . . and the watch to keep time. In that sense too it will be a 'happy watch' since it will be doing what fulfils it.

Our own human structure, and our corresponding loneliness, can be understood in a manner analogous to this. God is the good clockmaker, building our purpose right into our very structure. Thus, if we follow authentically our own inner dictates, laws and rhythms, we will naturally move towards that end for which we were made. Our own internal mechanisms will push us naturally towards meaning and fulfilment. In our case, however, the mainspring within our internal mechanism, that which causes the tension and ultimately causes our hands to move, is loneliness, a burning thirst for union with God, others, and the world. The very reason why God has made us is deeply imprinted into our very structure.

For Thomas, loneliness is the mainspring within our internal make-up. *Desiderium Naturale*, he calls it. Like the wound-up mainspring of a watch creates a tension which makes the watch's hands move, so too loneliness creates a tension inside of us which makes us move. It is the *raison d'être* of every action we do. We experience it at all levels within our being: *spiritually*, in our thirst for God; *aesthetically*, in our thirst for beauty; *psychologically*, in our desire for love and unity with others; *emotionally*, in our desire to feel a oneness with others and with all things; *intellectually*, in our thirst for knowledge and truth; and even *physically*, in our sexual tensions.

Loneliness, as we can see, is a very good and necessary force within our lives. It makes us tick. Much liberating insight can come from a proper understanding and self-appropriation of this.[10] We all go through life being too surprised at ourselves. Far too often we are surprised at the powerful tensions inside of us, surprised at the cataclysmic forces which often stir deep inside of our minds and bodies, surprised at our inability to be quiet and satisfied, surprised at the strength and unyieldingness of our sexual urges, and surprised simply at how much complexity and tension there is in being a human person. Thomas Aquinas was not surprised. Unlike Pascal, he did not marvel at the fact that a human person cannot sit quietly in his room. Furniture and ornaments can stay quietly in a room, their mainspring is not so tense and complex. They were built to stay in rooms. But when God made humans, he had a different purpose in mind and so he gave them a different mainspring, loneliness. To be human, then, is not to sit quietly in a room, but to be a searching lonely being, wandering from room to room, restlessly looking always for an all-consuming and infinite love and unity.

John of the Cross (AD 1542–1591)

Juan de Yepes y Alvarez, a sixteenth-century Spanish theologian and mystic, more commonly known as John of the Cross, also offers some valuable perspectives on loneliness. In his treatise, *The Living Flame of Love*, he summarises his theology of loneliness in three paragraphs:

The deep caverns of feeling,
These caverns are the soul's faculties: memory, intellect, and will. They are as deep as are the boundless goods of which they are capable, since anything less than the infinite fails to fill them. From what they suffer when they are empty, we can gain some knowledge of their enjoyment and delight when they are filled with God, since one contrary sheds light on the other.

In the first place, it is noteworthy that when these caverns of the faculties are not emptied, purged, and cleansed of every affection for creature, they do not feel the vast emptiness of their deep capacity. Any little thing that adheres to them in this life is sufficient to so burden and bewitch them that they do not perceive the harm, nor note the lack of their immense goods, nor know their own capacity.

It is an amazing thing that the least of these goods is enough so to encumber these faculties, capable of infinite goods, that they cannot receive these infinite goods until they are completely empty, as we shall see. Yet when these caverns are empty and pure, the thirst, hunger, and yearning of the spiritual feeling is intolerable. Since they have deep cavities they suffer profoundly, for the food they lack, which as I say is God, is also profound.[11]

Why are we lonely? What does our loneliness mean? For John, the answers to those questions are quite similar to those of Augustine and Thomas. His way of expression is different, but the analysis is essentially the same, namely, we are lonely because God built us that way.

John explains this by using the metaphor of 'caverns'. According to him, there are three constitutive faculties to each human person: intellect, will, and memory or mind, heart, and personality.[12] Each of these faculties is seen to be a cavern, a capacity of infinite depth – a 'grand canyon' without a bottom. As persons, we are so constituted that in our minds, hearts, and personalities, we are insatiable, bottomless wells, capable of receiving the infinite. God made us that way so that ultimately we could be in union with infinite love and life. Because of this, there can be no fully meaningful and ultimate solution to our loneliness outside union with the infinite. Therefore, in this life we are always lonely.

On these points John is very similar to Augustine and Thomas. His expatiation upon these points, however, produces some unique perspectives:

(1) *The immense danger of loneliness*

According to John, if our loneliness is not handled meaningfully and channelled creatively, it becomes a highly dangerous force within our lives. It leads to what he terms 'inordinate affectivity'[13] and a corresponding selfish and unhealthy pursuit of pleasure. This, as we saw earlier, can ultimately, if not recognised and checked, be destructive of our personality.[14]

(2) *In order to arrive at our real depth we must enter into our loneliness*

John has a very exalted notion of the human person. He sees each of us as a cavern of infinite depth, possessive of great sensitivity and of vast riches within our mind, heart, and personality. However, for him, the refusal to enter into our loneliness can condemn us to superficiality, to a life outside our own depth and richness. Again, he employs a metaphor to explain this.

For him, our mind, heart, and personality are analogous to bottomless canyons. But we can choose not to enter deeply into these canyons. We can let ourselves be frightened off and instead either cling to all kinds of things at the surface of our canyons or we can let ourselves be drawn away from our own depth by distracting activity. In either case we never enter deeply into ourselves. In either case, too, we end up living superficially and impoverished, drawing upon only a very small part of our own depth and richness.

What does that mean concretely? It means that, to the extent that we go through life running away from our own loneliness, we put a cellophane covering over our own depth and riches and live instead at the surface of our mind, heart, and personality. For John, this is probably the biggest problem that we face in dealing with our loneliness. We are too frightened of it to enter into it. The canyons of our mind and heart are so deep and so full of mystery that we try at all costs to avoid entering them deeply. We avoid journeying inward because we are too frightened; frightened because we must make that journey alone; frightened because we know it will involve solitude and perseverance; and frightened because we are entering the unknown. Aloneness, suffering, perseverance, the unknown, all these things frighten us. Our very own depths frighten us! And so we stall, distracting ourselves, drugging the pain, partying and travelling, keeping busy, trying this and trying that, clinging to people and moments, junking up the surface of our lives, and finding any and every excuse we can to avoid being alone and having to face ourselves. We are too frightened to travel inward. But we pay a price for that, a high one. Superficiality! So long as we avoid the painful journey inward, to the depth of our caverns, we live at the surface.

(3) *When we first do enter into our loneliness we enter into the pain of 'purgatory'*

John of the Cross, however, offers us no painless way to enter loneliness and to come to grips with it. He is very realistic here. The inward journey involves pain, intolerable pain. According to him, once we stop trying to run away from our loneliness, and stop trying to fill our thirsty caverns with counterfeit and pseudo solutions, we enter, for a time, into a terrible raging pain, the pain of purgatory, the pain which is felt when we cut ourselves off from pseudo-supports and take the plunge inward, into the infinite mystery of ourselves, reality, and God. Eventually this journey leads to a deep peace, but in the early stages it causes intolerable pain. Why?

Because we have stopped using anaesthetic. We have stopped numbing, drugging, distracting, and deflecting our lonely thirst. Thus, deprived of anaesthetic, and of the cellophane covering of superficiality, we can enter and feel fully our own depth. We face ourselves for the first time. Initially this is very painful. We begin to see ourselves as we truly are, infinite caverns, satiable only by the absolutely non-counterfeit, infinite love. We see too how, up to now, we have not drawn our strength and support from the infinite, but have drawn upon finite things. The realisation that we must shift our life-support system, and the process of that shift, is very painful. It is nothing other than the pain of purgatory,[15] the pain of withdrawal and the pain of birth. It is the pain of letting go of a life-support system which, however ineffectual, at least we could understand, and instead, in darkness, altruism, and hope moving out and trying to find life-support in the mystery of the infinite. It is a process of being born again, of having our present umbilical cord cut. Like all births it is a journey from the secure into the unknown; like all births it involves a certain death; and like all births, too, it is very painful because it is with much groaning of the flesh that new life is brought forth.

Karl Rahner (1904–1984)

The contemporary German theologian, Karl Rahner, is another important theological writer on the question of loneliness. Although he does not make an explicit treatise on loneliness, his highly developed theological anthropology logically and naturally extends itself to give many valuable healing insights into this problem. Perhaps more than any other contemporary theologian, Rahner helps render intelligible the phenomenon of loneliness and provides a theological basis for understanding loneliness.

How does he explain loneliness? His answer to that

question is contingent upon his theological anthropology in general. That anthropology (which is too complex to be explained in any detail here) can in a short and over-simplified way be expressed as follows:[16]

For him, any full explanation of the person must begin with God. In the beginning God was alone, but, wanting to share His infinite love and life, He posited for Himself a creature, the human being, with whom He could potentially share that life. We, as human persons, are therefore nothing other than possible partners that God has posited for Himself in order that He might share his life in dialogue, love, and beatific vision. Now, if we are to be capable of such a dialogical love relationship with an infinite God, this implies some pretty astonishing characteristics on our part. We must not only be free personal beings, capable of receiving and responding to such love and yet retaining our freedom and self-identity, but we must be *open to the infinite* as well, beings who are capable of receiving infinity itself in love and vision. Because of our capacity for the infinite, we are unable to achieve complete satisfaction and fulfilment in this life. We are by our very structure both blessed and condemned to be lonely and insatiable, restlessly striving to fill a space within ourselves which is infinitely deep.

In this sense, Rahner's explanation of the reason for, and the meaning of our loneliness, is almost identical with the explanations given by Augustine, Thomas, and John of the Cross. We are lonely because of the way God has made us, and our loneliness is very good, albeit painful, because it keeps us focused on the very purpose for which we were created. It is, however, in developing this anthropology that Rahner offers some unique perspectives on the question of loneliness.

(1) *Loneliness is co-extensive with our personality*

For Rahner, loneliness is not simply a part of our human nature, a restless thirst which is tacked on to an otherwise complete being. We are not beings who get lonely, but we *are* a loneliness (an 'Obediential Potency', he calls it).[17] We are a thirst, a capacity to receive infinite love, a potential to 'obediently' accept the divine life. Loneliness is not therefore a quality inherent in an otherwise complete person. It is so essential to our make-up that, viewed from a certain perspective, it can be seen to be the very constitutive element of our personality.[18]

(2) *Loneliness motivates us and makes us dynamic beings*

Rahner defines the human person as 'Obediential Potency', as having the capacity to receive and respond freely to infinite love and life. Moreover, he sees the human person as dynamic rather than static capacity, that is, our capacity to receive infinite life is not something to which we can be indifferent (as a pail can be indifferent to the fact that it has a capacity to hold water). Instead we have a capacity which makes itself dynamically felt (as a burning desire for water makes itself felt in a thirsty man). Loneliness is simply the felt experience of our 'Obediential Potency'. In our loneliness, 'in the torment of the insufficiency of everything attainable',[19] we experience our nature, learn the reason why God had made us, and are pushed out of ourselves in order to move towards that end.

Hence our loneliness is ultimately what motivates us. The inner dynamism of our mind, heart, and physical faculties pushes us outwards, constantly forcing us to keep striving to attain absolute love and knowledge. We are constantly being driven by our loneliness to seek more love, more knowledge, and more beauty. We have an inbuilt loneliness which makes us longing, yearning, grasping, and hungry creatures. Our aspirations for love and knowledge are limitless, yet our capability of fulfilling these aspirations is always limited, no matter how good a situation we are in. For this reason we are, this side of heaven, always somewhat lonely.

However, the fact that our loneliness is really our

striving for infinite love and life is not something which we are usually *explicitly* conscious of as a search for the absolute. *Explicitly*, we are generally only aware that we are lonely, and that we want some particular person, experience, or object, or some group of persons, experiences, or objects. However, *implicitly* even when we are seeking some very particular person, experience, or object, we are actually striving to attain God. Our loneliness always points us towards God.[20] A rather poignant, though unfortunately not uncommon example, will help to illustrate what is meant here.

Imagine, for instance, a lonely man on a Saturday night. Restless and unable to satisfy himself by reading or watching television, he heads out, looking for some action. He cruises the night spots for a while and eventually ends up in a bar. A few drinks and a few hours later, he returns home in the company of a prostitute with whom he spends the night and with whom he tries to alleviate his loneliness. His explicit motive may have been anything but spiritual, yet a proper understanding of loneliness points out the deepest reason for his quest. However perverted his search may have become, that man is looking for God! His fundamental loneliness still has the same meaning. He is restlessly and desperately being driven by his own inner dynamisms to look for infinite love and life. Like all persons, he has been made with a heart that is lonely and thirsty for God's kingdom, for union within the body of Christ. Furtive union with a prostitute is simply a perverted and futile attempt to fill that gap. Like all persons, this man was created hungry, so that he might desire to eat the bread of life. In restless desperation, unable to recognise the authentic bread from heaven, he has tried an unfulfilling substitute.

What does all this mean concretely? It means that, given such an understanding of loneliness, we should not be so surprised that we go through life restless and unable to sit still. Also, knowing how central loneliness is to our personality structure, we should not be so surprised at

how perverted and desperate attempts to fill that emptiness can be. Above all, though, such an understanding of
loneliness should help liberate us. It should teach us that
loneliness is both a very good and a very natural force in
our lives. Being lonely does not mean that we are abnormal, love-starved, over-sexed, or alienated. Perhaps all it
means is that we are incurably human and sensitive to the
fact that God made us for an ecstatic togetherness in a
body with Himself and with all other persons of sincere
will. Loneliness is simply our hunger for that. Our sexuality, our physical loneliness, is also part of that. A proper
understanding of loneliness should aid us to direct our
lonely impulses creatively and correctly in order to move
towards the goal for which we were made. If listened to
correctly, loneliness keeps telling us the purpose for which
God made us. This implies the giving up of false messianic
expectations. There can be no final solution to our loneliness in this life. No amount of partying and drinking,
pleasure and travel, fame and fortune, success or creativity, indeed no amount of genuine human love and affection, can ever fully take our loneliness away. All these
things are good in themselves and can even help somewhat to alleviate our loneliness. But God has made us
bigger than all that. Yes, even bigger than human love
and affection! Only a total all-encompassing consummate
union with all sincere persons and with the divine life
itself will finally put to rest our last lonely impulse.

THE POTENTIAL VALUE OF LONELINESS

Loneliness: danger and opportunity

The Chinese word for *crisis* is made up of two characters: one stands for *danger*, the other for *opportunity*. Few analogies are as apt as this one to describe the potential influence of loneliness in our lives. Like every crisis, it comes laden with both immense dangers and immense opportunities. We have already seen how potentially dangerous loneliness can be. It is time now to look at the tremendous opportunities for growth that it offers us, if it is understood and channelled creatively.

The hidden benefits: the potential value of loneliness

(1) *Loneliness can be helpful in spurring us on towards both greater commitment and greater creativity*

Our loneliness can be a very positive force in that, if listened to correctly, it can help lead us continually towards greater depth of commitment in giving ourselves for others and for causes greater than ourselves. Dag Hammarskjold, one of the giants of our century, once put it this way: 'Pray that your loneliness may spur you towards finding something to live for, that's great enough to die for.'[1] Very often it is precisely in our loneliness that we learn that there is something greater than ourselves, that our own world and our own concerns are not all that there is and that we are called to give ourselves for others.

Why is that? Why can we not come to recognise these things and commit ourselves to something greater than ourselves, without the necessity of the pain of loneliness? Because in our day-to-day lives, when all is well, and health, friends, inner peace, and good cheer are in abundance, we tend to lose our awareness of reality as it really is. We tend to become selfish and self-centred, making the world revolve around ourselves, forgetting that we live in a world in which we are interdependent with millions of others, and that we are partly responsible for helping that world and others reach a common goal. We tend to forget, and pretty easily too, that our world is flawed and unfinished, that we have work to do, and that our life is not our own to use selfishly. Put crassly, when times are good, and we are not lonely, we tend to worry more about our boat and our next vacation to Hawaii, than about the wounds that bleed unattended and uncared for in our unfinished world. But, when we are lonely, when we have to come face to face with emptiness and lack of meaning, we are given a great opportunity to understand life and ourselves. We have to react, as Karl Jaspers once put it, either by obfuscation or by despair and rebirth.[2] In either case we are forced, almost against our will, to understand life more deeply.

Loneliness, perhaps more than any other single force, can help mature us and help make us less selfish. It offers us the route to rebirth, to a birth into a life beyond our own self-enclosed world, because it offers us an opportunity to connect ourselves and our task to the task of all humanity. In loneliness, we can all find something to live for, that's great enough to die for! Reflecting on what led him to his own commitment, Dag Hammarskjold remarked: 'I don't know who – or what – put the question, I don't know when it was put. I don't even remember answering. But at some moment I did answer yes to someone – or something – and from that hour I was certain that existence is meaningful and that, therefore, my life, in self-surrender, had a goal.'[3] In our loneliness, we hear the question.

Loneliness can also spur us on to new heights of creativity. It is no secret that many of our greatest works of literature, art, poetry, music, and philosophy arose from the depths of someone's loneliness. Human creativity can, in many ways, be compared to a meteorological phenomenon: no star was ever born, except that there first existed a burning chaos. And it is almost trite to mention that there never was a rainbow without there first having been rain.

I would like to illustrate this by using as an example a very creative person of the past century, Soren Kierkegaard, the father of modern existentialism. A gifted and prolific writer, Kierkegaard always saw his own loneliness as a creative pain, something almost to be deliberately cultivated and nurtured. For him, living in loneliness was part of a vocation from God. For this reason, among others, he refused marriage, even though he was deeply in love with someone. He sacrificed, as he saw it, married love so that he could continue his vocation of loneliness. Many of his works arose out of his own loneliness and, for that exact reason, speak deeply healing words to many of us who read him. His words are liberating for many persons, not because they contain great truths, hitherto unknown, but because they issue forth from the depths of a lonely heart and therefore can speak to the depth of other hearts.[4]

Kierkegaard once wrote: 'What is a poet? An unhappy man who conceals deep torments in his heart, but whose lips are so formed that when a groan or a shriek streams out over them it sounds like beautiful music.'[5] This was the way he saw himself: a man bound to loneliness, but whose lips and words tried to form that pain into beautiful music – music which could bring healing to those who hear it. Thousands of other artists and poets see themselves in a similar way. From the depth of lonely pain issues forth much creativity.

In her best-seller, *The Thorn Birds*, Colleen McCullough employs a very rich and penetrating metaphor. She begins the book with a legend about a bird which sings only once in its life. This bird, called the *thorn bird*, from the instant it leaves its nest begins to hunt for a thorn tree. When it finds one, it impales itself upon the longest thorn. Then, in the pain of being so pierced, and dying, it sings a song so beautiful that the whole world stops to listen, and God in heaven smiles.[6] This metaphor alone is sufficient to explain the astounding popularity of this book. As it suggests, when the pain of our own loneliness pierces the very deepest and tenderest part of our heart, we, writhing in pain, might for once in our life sing a song so beautiful that the whole world will stop and listen, and God will smile. From the fiery chaos inside us we can give birth to a star.

(2) *Loneliness can help us to become more understanding and empathetic*

John of the Cross once said that the value of loneliness and solitude is that it makes us 'mild, bringing the mild into harmony with the mild'.[7] How right he was! Few things in life help create as much mildness, understanding, and empathy inside us as does loneliness. Mystics, contemplatives, poets, philosophers, and sensitive persons of all kinds have continually pointed this out to us, telling us how, in the experience of our own troubled and lonely hearts, we can come to understanding and empathy, because we can recognise there both the threads that can bind human community, and the forces which can drive it apart. In understanding our own heart, with all its complexities and ambiguities, noble aspirations and altruistic capabilities, and with all its potential malice and greed, we come to understand more fully each other and the world we live in. Empathy and understanding are born in the deepest and loneliest spot inside us, for it is there that what is most personal in us is also most universal. We understand others, when we understand ourselves. A professor of mine used to say: 'Lonely is the person who understands!' How true! Yet the reverse is equally as true and poignant: 'The lonely person understands!'

Many recent books have spoken deeply and sensitively about this.[8] Henri Nouwen speaks for all when he writes:

> It is in the solitude of the heart that we can truly listen to the pains of the world because there we can recognize them not as strange and unfamiliar pains, but as pains which are indeed our own. There I can see that what is most universal is most personal and that indeed nothing human is strange to me. There I can see that Hiroshima, My-Lai, Attica, and Watergate are realities of the human heart, my own included, and that to protest first of all asks for a testimony of my own participation in the human condition. There I can indeed respond.[9]

Robert Frost, in his poem 'Mending Wall' wrote:

> Before I built a wall, I'd ask to know
> What I was walling in or walling out,
> And to whom I was like to give offense.
> Something there is that doesn't love a wall,
> That wants it down.[10]

All of us want community, understanding and empathy. There is something in us all that doesn't love a wall, that wants it down! Yet unless each of us makes that painful inward journey and, grappling with our loneliness, learns that what is most personal to us is also most universal, we will continue to believe in the need for walls, and not knowing exactly what we are walling in or walling out, we will continue to build them. Then, not being able to fully understand others because we do not fully understand ourselves, we will continue to live in fear and prejudice, defensiveness and suspicion, throwing up walls wherever possible.

(3) *Loneliness can be a force which helps sensitise us to the needs and yearnings of our heart*

In a hit song, 'Sit down young stranger', singer-composer Gordon Lightfoot tells the story of a young man's wanderings and his search for meaning. Describing both the happy and sad times, he says: 'Sometimes it could get lonely, but it taught me how to cry!' Loneliness, among its many benefits, can teach us how to cry, and that is no small thing.

Earlier in this book we were introduced to Hagar Shipley, the tragic heroine of Margaret Laurence's *Stone Angel*. Unable to bring herself to tears, poor Hagar lived and died in the unforgivable sin against the Holy Spirit, a pride that would not relent. Had she been able to let her pride give way to tears, redemptive love and life would have flowed into her, giving meaning to both her life and death.

Loneliness can do that for us. It can teach us how to cry and, by that very fact, sensitise us to all that is deepest, softest, and most worthwhile inside of ourselves. Because redemption is built upon tears, loneliness is helpful in leading us to redemption. Let me explain this by comparing two persons: Studs Lonigan, of James T. Farrell's great novel *Studs Lonigan*[11] and Caleb, the 'Cain' figure of John Steinbeck's *East of Eden*.[12] Their different response to loneliness, and their ability or inability to cry, makes the difference between redemption and damnation of a continued existence in loneliness.

Studs Lonigan is the story of the development of one person, William Lonigan, from the time he is a very young boy until his death in early adulthood. William is called 'Studs' by his friends because he is tough.

Tough is indeed the only word which fittingly describes him. Growing up in a rough neighbourhood in Chicago at the turn of the century, Studs is the toughest of the tough. He is the fighter, the drinker, the man who prefers the whorehouse to marriage, a good time in the poolroom to family life. Hard as rock, there are no soft spots to him. There is no loneliness inside of him. He lives fast, and for himself. Others may cry and snivel, but never Studs; he is his own man, knowing how to take care of himself. One need not look his way if one expects to see human tears!

That is how others see Studs Lonigan. That is also how he likes to see himself, namely, as having no vulnerability, no real need of others, as being totally in control. However, there is another side to Studs. Sometimes when he is by himself, and is stripped of the need to play a role, his need for others and his need to be soft impales itself upon him, slipping through his armour of toughness. He teeters on the edge of redemptive tears, on the edge of admitting his vulnerability and loneliness. Unfortunately, he never falls into tears. The tough overcomes the soft, and William remains Studs. Also, twice he falls in love with a girl. But both times that love which might have brought him out of himself is frustrated by his own unwillingness to be vulnerable. As a result, Studs wins out over William, the tough guy wins out over the real person, and, when he dies tragically of pneumonia at age thirty-eight, Studs Lonigan is a very alienated and lonely man, a man who has never cried, but a man who has never really loved either.

A tragic and pathetic story, surely! Yet there is more than a little bit of Studs Lonigan in each of us. How often do we masquerade as the tough one, the invulnerable one, the unlonely one, the one who never cries? Yet underneath it all we remain ever the scared and lonely little boys and girls we have always been. We are not so tough after all. All we really want is that others love and accept us. The tough-guy façade fools no one, least of all ourselves. Our power trips and our propensity to send out signals that we are not lonely and vulnerable, are really only our desperate way of telling others how badly we need them. Hopefully our story will not end like Studs Lonigan's, nor like Hagar Shipley's. Perhaps our loneliness will teach us how to cry and then our story can end like Caleb Trask's.[13]

Caleb Trask is the real hero of John Steinbeck's *East of Eden*. Even though he and his twin brother, Aaron, do not appear in the first two-thirds of the book, the story is really about them. Their father, Adam Trask, is a lonely and loving man. Their mother, Cathy (later called Kate), is a prostitute who deserts their father and them at their birth.

Right from the beginning of their lives, Caleb and Aaron resemble Cain and Abel. Aaron is Abel. Fair-haired and good-looking, likeable by nature, he is everyone's favourite, especially his father's. Virtue and goodness seemingly come naturally to him, and all he does seems to please people. Caleb is Cain. Darker in complexion, quiet and naturally withdrawn, he is less able to make friends. People seem to naturally shy away from him. He is, from early age, a loner, a man with a certain darkness about him.

Seemingly stigmatised by nature, Caleb feels lonely and rejected. At first he lets these painful feelings drive him to meanness. He tries to hurt others, especially Aaron; however, he always feels cheap and guilty whenever he does this.

One day he learns the story concerning his mother, how she had deserted them at birth, and how she is now a prostitute, living in the same town as he does. With this discovery, which he keeps from Aaron, his love for his father suddenly deepens. In a burst of first-fervour, he hits upon a scheme to raise five thousand dollars to give as a gift to his father, who had recently lost that amount in an unsuccessful business venture. His scheme is successful, and as the time approaches to give his father the gift, he becomes very nervous and excited, wondering how his father will react.

Sadly, his father rejects his gift. Even in the face of a gift like this, his father prefers Aaron to him. Like Cain's gift was rejected in favour of Abel's, so too was Caleb's rejected in favour of his brother.

Hurt and angry, Caleb goes out for a walk and meets his

brother. He tells Aaron that he would like to show him something and, in a spiteful mood, takes him to see his mother. This visit is too much for both Kate and Aaron. Both are broken by the trauma of it. After their visit, Kate commits suicide, leaving her money to Aaron. Aaron, after knocking down Caleb, runs off and joins the army. Caleb, on his part, gets drunk and, the next day, burns the money he had offered as a gift to his father.

Sometime later, a telegram arrives informing their father that Aaron has been killed in the war. Adam, upon hearing this, has a severe stroke. The burden of his brother's death and his father's sickness now falls on Caleb. That weight is too much for him: he realises that this guilt will crush him. He fears that for the rest of his life he will be unable to avoid seeing his father's eyes, staring at him and telling him that he has killed his brother.

But unlike his biblical counterpart, Cain, who spends the rest of his life wandering over the face of the earth, stigmatised by his guilt and unable to escape hearing the cry of his dying brother, Caleb seeks redemption instead. Guilty and crushed by the loneliness and the darkness inside of himself, he cries. He asks to be accepted and forgiven.

His father is on his deathbed when Caleb enters, seeking forgiveness. Adam, with great effort, whispers *timshel*, a Hebrew word which gives a choice, *thou mayest*. In using this word, he is letting Caleb know that the way is open, the choice is his.

The novel ends on a positive note. Contrary to Cain, contrary to Studs Lonigan, contrary to Hagar Shipley, and contrary to all the odds against him, Caleb opens his heart to love and forgiveness. Spurred on by his own loneliness and guilt, he chooses to seek love and forgiveness over the temptation to become bitter and calloused. Redemption comes with his tears. As the novel ends, we feel assured that, like his biblical namesake, Caleb, he too will reach the promised land.

Loneliness can teach us to cry. That is no small favour. Like Caleb Trask, in our loneliness, we are given the chance to turn bitterness into tears, guilt into the desire for forgiveness. When that happens, redemption is usually not far off.

(4) *Loneliness, if listened to, puts pressure on us to pay the price of love, that is, self-sacrifice*

Loneliness serves us, too, in that it continually puts pressure on us to pay the price of real love. Real love, that is, altruistic love, the type described by Jesus and the New Testament, does not come naturally to us. Nobody falls into love! Love is always the result of some effort and some sacrifice, of some bleeding and some crying. It is the result of some willingness on a person's part to be hung up on a cross and to die a little. Only three types of persons think that real love is easy: those who are already *saints*, who through long years of painful practice have made love a habit; *manipulators*, who have confused their own self-gratification with genuine love; and *unrealistic dreamers*, who do not know what they are talking about. Tainted as we are by our own self-concern, genuine love is very hard to attain, and especially to sustain.

The experience of loneliness, though, can be a tremendous aid to us in our struggle to leave self and go towards others – with altruistic love. Very often it is only because we suffer loneliness that we are willing to make the necessary effort and sacrifice that the harsh dictates of love demand.

Imagine, for example, a little boy playing ball with his friends in the playground. Pampered and spoiled at home, he refuses to follow the rules of the game, but instead bends everything to suit his own selfish whims. Eventually frustrated by his self-centredness, the other kids leave him to himself and go off to play elsewhere. Bitter and hurt, he sits pouting for a time, blaming the other kids for his own misery. But it gets pretty lonely sitting and pouting (as we have all learned) and so eventually he swallows his pride (and perhaps has a good cry as well) and returns to play with the others. This time, however, he agrees to be less selfish and to play by the rules. He has learned a few lessons about loving which perhaps, barring the experience of rejection and loneliness, he might never have learned.

If we never got lonely, it would be all too easy to become selfish. We could, at any time it suited us, go into a shell of bitterness, pride, self-pity, selfishness, and the like. The experience of loneliness, though, makes it difficult for us to spin this type of cocoon around ourselves. By causing us pain and making us uncomfortable, loneliness helps pressure us into breaking down many of the barriers of selfishness and pride which prevent us from relating to God and others in a real loving way.

Loneliness, when boiled down to its roots, is nothing other than a thirst for love. This thirst, because it is so strong and unquenchable, puts constant pressure on us to pay the price for communication and love. It is a dynamism operative within us, forcing us to work at making ourselves more lovable.

(5) *Loneliness is God's way of drawing us towards the end for which He made us, namely, union with Himself and our fellow human beings*

Loneliness is not something at the fringes of our lives, which we can ignore at will. It is a dimension of our self-awareness, something co-extensive with our personalities. We exist in the world as lonely beings, as thirsty and yearning at all levels of our persons. Our bodies are lonely, our minds are lonely, and our very souls are lonely. But what are they lonely for?

Looked at superficially, our loneliness is often seen as being either directed towards a very specific person, object, or experience, or as being too inchoate to be focused on anything definite or particular. Loneliness is seldom seen as having a generic aim; either it is seen as having a very specific aim, or it is seen as having no aim whatever. However, looked at sensitively and through the eyes of faith, we see that our loneliness has a very clear generic aim. We are thirsty for love and community, for unity with God and others in a body, the body of Christ. Loneliness is God's way of drawing us into that body.

Through Scripture and the tradition of Christianity, God tells us explicitly what He wants for us. However, it is easy to ignore His voice as it speaks to us through these media. Our loneliness, however, forces us to hear a voice we cannot ignore. Through the burning thirst of our spirit, and the erotic urges of our body, we are literally propelled outward to seek unity and community.

Thus, loneliness can be seen as God's way of drawing us towards Himself. Like the Psalmist, in loneliness, we constantly experience the pull towards the infinite:

> God, you are my God, I am seeking you,
> my soul is thirsting for you,
> my flesh is longing for you,
> a land parched, weary and waterless.[14]

Also, in loneliness, God draws us towards each other, towards a oneness in the body of Christ. We can come to understand this simply by examining sensitively and honestly the pain of our own loneliness. When we do this, we see that the pain of our lonely eroticism is not so inchoate and lacking in generic direction after all. Rather it is the pain which results from our not being in complete intimacy with everyone. It is the pain of unconsummated love, the pain of not being fully within the body of Christ. Loneliness is our thirst for heaven, for the real heaven. Unfortunately, we do not always relate our loneliness to this because, too frequently, we conceive of heaven as a static, lifeless, dematerialised, desexualised, and generally inhuman place, where we will live in disembodied boredom, contemplating in some platonic way the mysteries and grandeur of God. Our loneliness is God's magnet, pulling us towards the real heaven, the one Jesus and the mystics have told us about, that is, the kingdom of love and togetherness in which we will live in an all-in-one-flesh unity, in the unity of a body, Christ's body, in which all love and longing will come to perfect consummation in a radical and ecstatic spiritual, psychological, emotional, physical, and yes, even sexual, togetherness. As so many mystics have put it, heaven will be the wedding night. All longing for unity will be a thing of the past.[15]

Our loneliness, then, because it is our thirst for heaven, can be an extremely good and important force in our lives. God has made us in such a way that we yearn, at all levels of our being, for warmth and community in Christ's body. This, perhaps more than any other single force, can motivate us to move out of ourselves to seek warmth and community.

Moreover, given this understanding of loneliness, it is no wonder that we go through life lonely and restless. Ultimately destined to come together in an ecstatic all-in-one-flesh unity with God and each other, it is not so surprising that, as we journey through life, we hunger for this along the way.

(6) *Loneliness can help lead us to make a commitment of faith*

Loneliness can, and very often does, lead us to make a deeper commitment of faith. By depriving us of any lasting satisfaction in our experience of finite things, loneliness forces us constantly to search for something deeper, more fulfilling, more all-encompassing, and more lasting than what we are presently experiencing. If not deadened through anaesthetics or deflected through distracting activity, loneliness will constantly lead us to the edge of real faith.

Reading through autobiographies and biographies of

various saints, mystics, and other great persons, we see that in many cases these people were literally pushed to their knees by their own restlessness and loneliness. We see that, while they tried to avoid the hound of heaven at all costs, again and again they were eventually caught by him in their loneliness. Loneliness was the crack through which he slipped in. It was there, in the lonely spaces of their minds and hearts, where truth can sear the soul, that they were forced to choose. Faith or despair?

In loneliness, we are afforded no neutral ground upon which we can exist peacefully, but selfishly. We are forced to either genuflect before something greater than ourselves or we are forced into despair and self-destructive activity. In loneliness we see the truth.

At one stage of Christ's ministry, the novelty of His message begins to wear off, and His listeners begin to see the real meaning and implication of His teachings. Most of His followers become disenchanted and leave Him at this stage. His closest disciples, too, are tempted to leave, but, when Jesus asks them: 'What about you, do you want to go away too?' Peter answers: 'Lord to whom shall we go?'[16] Our loneliness can be a big help in bringing each of us to say similar words to Christ.

The act of faith is not easy to make. It demands, among other things, that we gamble real life on hope, that we give up what we already possess, see, and understand, for something which we do not yet possess, see, or understand. It is not easy, nor natural, to make the leap of faith, to learn to live life and draw support from that which is beyond what we can experience naturally. Yet, in our loneliness, in the torment of the insufficiency of everything attainable, we are forced to stand on the precipice of secure existence, and to look over the edge. And, even though we cannot clearly see what is beyond that edge we stand on, we are given some help in taking the leap into the unknown.

(7) *Loneliness can teach us that we are pilgrims on earth.*

The gospel teaches us that we live in an age and a world which is unfinished, which is still journeying towards full redemption. It teaches us that we are pilgrims on earth. Our life, therefore, is supposed to be characterised by pilgrimage, by travel. Like the ten virgins of the gospel parable,[17] we are supposed to be journeying towards our wedding night, with all else relativised because of our anticipation of the coming consummation. And we are supposed to be travelling light, with lamps lit. Sometimes we forget this, and like the five foolish virgins let our lamps go out, ensconce ourselves, collect some permanent furniture. Instead of living in anticipation of our wedding, we try to cram the optimum amount of pleasure and experience into the few years of earthly life we have, as if the bridegroom were not going to come. When we do this, we do violence to ourselves, others, and the very plan which God has for our happiness. We are not meant to live as comfortably ensconced citizens, listening to a finished symphony, in an eternal city. We are pilgrims, engaged young ladies on the way to our wedding, travelling light, and refusing to buy any permanent furniture.

However, we so easily forget this. The bridegroom seems to be in no particular hurry to come, and so the temptation is constant: let the lamps go out, unpack, and settle in! For this reason, the pain of our loneliness can be an immense aid to us. By keeping us in a perennial state of restlessness and dissatisfaction, it helps prevent us from, precisely, unpacking and settling in. It reminds us of the wedding, keeps us longing for the bridegroom, and helps us see that the various offers of permanent residency and permanent furniture are less than fully satisfying. As soon as we start unpacking to move in, our loneliness and restlessness make us eager again for the journey. If the five foolish virgins had listened sensitively to their own loneliness, they would never have let their lamps go out! If listened to, the pain of loneliness teaches us, as Karl

Rahner so aptly puts it, that here in this life 'all symphonies remain unfinished'.[18] Thus, loneliness can teach us our true condition as human beings.

Paradoxically, the realisation that we are pilgrims on earth is both very painful and very liberating. On the one hand, it is painful because it forces us to meet life realistically, to put our face to the wind, and to give up many of our false dreams and unrealistic expectations. There is always a certain amount of painful stoicism required in doing this. On the other hand though, the realisation and existential acceptance of our pilgrim status is also very liberating because, through this, we can learn how to appreciate more fully the gift-dimension of life. Through loneliness we are taught to accept life with the reverence and respect it merits. An illustration will help explain this.

In the movie, *The Trial of Billy Jack*, there is a sequence in which Billy is on trial before a hostile courtroom. He realises that his life is in danger, but he is unafraid and unruffled as he faces this possibility. He tells the courtroom part of his secret:

'When you get up every morning, ask yourself, "If I died today, how important would the things I am going to do today really be?" By doing this you will see the relative unimportance of so many of your daily tasks and preoccupations. But then, go further and ask yourself: "But if I did die today, what would I want to do during my last day?" In all likelihood you would want to do many of the things you usually do. Therefore you see how precious they really are. You see, in relativizing your life and your work and preoccupations, you see both their unimportance and their preciousness.'[19]

The realisation of our pilgrim status can help bring us this type of awareness. By realising that we are only journeying on this earth for a short time, we learn to see the relative and transitory nature of all our relationships, activities, and preoccupations in this life. Paradoxically, however, this leads us to see them not in a stoic fashion, but for what they really are, a tremendous undeserved gift. Only when we sense that something is given to us but for a short time do we fully realise its gift-dimension. If, indeed, we knew that we were to die tomorrow, we would, on this our last day, quickly come to the realisation of how precious are the gifts of life, friendship, love, health, and work.

All is precious gift. This realisation is important because we too frequently go through life taking things and persons for granted. Life, friendship, health, and work, are seen as things which are *owed* to us. For this precise reason we fail to appreciate them and accept them with the reverence and respect they deserve. Instead of seeing them for what they are, precious gifts, we take them for granted, over-expect from them, over-demand from them, and generally abuse and use them in a fashion which leaves little room for reverence and respect. Then, having lost the sense of the gift-dimension of our life and friendships, we wonder why we are so petty and greedy, exploitative and manipulative, bitter and self-pitying. If we were ever reduced to having only that which we actually deserve, and like Job found ourselves on a dung-heap, deprived of our health and possessing nothing, we would see, in that poverty, how much of our life and love, health and joy, come to us as undeserved gifts. Once we learn that we are pilgrims on earth then suddenly our life becomes a lot less 'ordinary' and humdrum. Suddenly family members and other persons who care for us, but whom we have long taken for granted and stopped respecting and appreciating fully, become a lot more precious. A wit once remarked: 'Be it ever so humdrum, there is no rut like your own!' A pilgrim traveller avoids falling into a rut. For her there is no such thing as an 'ordinary' or humdrum experience. She takes nothing for granted. Rather, enthusiastic about the people she is meeting and the places she is seeing, she is constantly taking pictures and storing up precious memories. The realisation that we are pilgrims goes a long way in teaching us to meet life

with the reverence it merits because it makes us see life
for what it really is, a precious undeserved gift.

An acceptance of our pilgrim status also has the effect of
teaching us not to over-expect in relationships. Once we
accept the fact that we are pilgrims, and stop trying to
reap (and at times, rape) from life enough pleasure and
happiness to fill every empty spot inside of us, then for the
first time we will be free enough to stop looking at each
new friend and experience as possibly 'messianic', as a
possible final solution here in this life, that our symphony
will have to remain partly unfinished. As a result, we no
longer demand from others what they cannot give us,
namely, a full solution to our loneliness. This can go a long
way in helping us to respect others more fully.

Loneliness, if sensitively listened to, can help teach us
what it means to live in the interim eschatological age,
that time between Christ's first coming and His return at
the end of time to consummate His kingdom. By keeping
us perennially restless and dissatisfied, loneliness, like
many other things – living in community, reading God's
word, breaking bread together, challenging and consoling
each other, and re-enacting through ritual the major
saving words and events of Christ's life – helps keep alive
in us Christ's promise that, on a certain day, He will
return, break open the seventh seal, and dry every tear
upon the face of the earth.

(8) *Loneliness is an invitation to share in the*
    loneliness of Jesus.

Our loneliness, too, has value in that it is an invitation
given to us to share in the redemptive loneliness of Jesus.
As scholars and mystics have always pointed out to us, the
loneliness of Jesus was an important part of His redemptive act. He redeemed us not just by teaching and doing
miracles, but also, and especially, by His suffering and His
loneliness. It is not too strong to say: by His loneliness we
have been healed and made one.[20]

Today we help form Christ's body and presence on earth. The Incarnation is not an experiment which ended when Christ ascended. God is still incarnate in Christ, in us. It is up to us to actualise Christ's presence on earth. And, we must actualise the *whole* Christ: His word, His healing powers, His reconciliation, His death and resurrection, and His loneliness. Just as the passion and crucifixion of Christ continue until the end of the world in those who suffer, so too the loneliness of Christ continues in all those who are lonely.[21]

Our own loneliness, then, is an invitation to help keep incarnate the lonely ministry of Christ. In our own loneliness we are asked to weep with Him over Jerusalem, sweat lonely tears with Him in the garden, battle the forces of Satan in the desert, and, from a cross somewhere, cry out with Him in anguish at a silent God.

After the Second World War, the following words were found written on the wall of a Nazi concentration camp:

> I believe in the sun, even when it isn't shining,
> I believe in love, even when I feel it not,
> I believe in God, even when He is silent.

Our loneliness is an invitation from God to make those words our own and, by so doing, help keep incarnate in this world the redemptive passion and death of Christ.

TOWARDS A SPIRITUALITY OF LONELINESS

No instant solutions

Knowing that loneliness admits of various types and that it can be potentially a very creative force in our lives is, in itself, already valuable. However, that is only the first step in creatively coming to grips with it; handling it creatively requires more than this. What is required is something beyond a mere intellectual understanding of this force with all its various meanings and its potential dangers and advantages. To handle loneliness in a creative fashion requires a *certain way of living*. Within our lives we must develop, through much hard effort and long painful struggle, certain patterns of life which will help us to cope with the pain of loneliness, and which will help us to turn its potentially paralysing grip into a creative force. What is needed is a spirituality of loneliness: a spirituality which differentiates among the various types of loneliness and offers certain directions within which we can move in order to turn it into a creative rather than a destructive force within our lives.

What follows is an attempt, however rudimentary and scant, to point in the direction within which such a spirituality might be found.[1]

Handling 'alienation-loneliness': in search of integration

Few things are as painful to us as is 'alienation-loneliness' since all of us, in varying degrees, are frustrated by our lack of intimacy with others. We talk much about love and sharing, perhaps more than about anything else. Yet, when we try to really exchange love, sometimes in considerable desperation, we are seldom very successful. We are a bunch of lonely persons, desperately trying to love each other, but more often than not, we are not succeeding very well.

How is this 'alienation-loneliness' to be overcome? By a movement towards a fuller integration of ourselves into the lives and the world of others. Intimacy lies there, beyond the borders of our own lives. But how is this to be achieved? This movement, from 'alienation-loneliness' to integration, is not something we can accomplish overnight. It is achieved according to degrees, namely, according to the degree that we can move ever more deeply within the direction of greater risk, greater vulnerability, greater giving of free space, greater playfulness, and a greater giving of ourselves for crucifixion:

(1) *Risk*[2]

One of the greatest forces which serves to keep us in isolation from each other is fear. All of us are imprisoned, to a greater or lesser extent, by a bad self-image and a sense of shame which keep us living in fear, fear of many things. Mainly we fear that we are unlovable, that others will reject us, and that we are not good enough. We are also ashamed: ashamed of our own bodies, ashamed of the dark corners of our minds, and ashamed of our very persons. So we are, all of us, cautious persons, always most careful to weigh all the angles before risking opening ourselves within relationships.

We are not strong enough, nor self-confident enough,

nor sure enough of our own lovableness to risk putting ourselves on the line. The fear of being rejected is so great within us that we would sooner not make ourselves available to love than present ourselves honestly and openly and risk being rejected. We would sooner live in loneliness than risk getting hurt.

And so we go through life never really revealing how we truly feel, and how much we really care. Because of fear and shame, we play games. We play at being strong, at being cool, at being self-sufficient. We play at not telling others how badly we really need them. How often in our lives does fear, of whatever kind, prevent us from telling someone how we really feel about him/her? How often does fear of being rejected prevent us from moving openly and freely towards a relationship we would dearly love to have? How often do we leave it to the other, or to circumstance, to initiate or deepen a relationship we desperately want?

We are all pretty timid, really! We live in fear and shame. Sometimes these feelings are not recognised, or they are disguised and paraded as self-confidence, boisterousness, or aggressiveness. But they are always there, preventing us from being free persons, keeping us locked in alienation and loneliness.

Accordingly, one of the first things we need to do, if we wish to move towards greater intimacy with others, is to risk more. Only when we risk enough to let someone hurt us, are we risking enough to let someone love us. When we make ourselves available enough to be hurt, we will finally be available enough to be truly loved. We must, despite our fear and shame, and despite the fact that we might be rejected and hurt, reach out. We must constantly force ourselves to greater honesty and openness within relationships. We must constantly force ourselves to leave less to circumstance and to tell others how much we do care, and how much they really do mean to us.

Whenever we feel the pain of 'alienation-loneliness', whenever we are frustrated by our lack of intimacy with others, one of the first areas on which we must examine ourselves is the area of risking within relationships. Are we risking enough? Are we too afraid of being rejected? Are we playing games? Are we perhaps so cautious within relationships that we are not available enough to be loved?

It is risky to expose ourselves in friendship and love. At times we will make fools of ourselves, at times we will be rejected, and at times we will get hurt. However, most times our honesty and vulnerability will meet with acceptance, gratitude, and a counter-offer of a deeper friendship and a more satisfying intimacy.

(2) *Vulnerability* [3]

One of the greatest obstacles to intimacy is the propensity that we all have to believe that others will love us only when we are impressive and strong. It is because of this that we go through life trying to impress others into liking us. Rather than showing ourselves to each other as we really are, vulnerable, tender, and lovable, we are constantly trying to be so sensational that others have to love us. Like the inhabitants of the ancient city of Babel, we are constantly trying to build towers impressive enough to overpower others into loving us. This, the refusal to be vulnerable, is one of the greatest causes of loneliness. It is because of this refusal to be vulnerable that, far too often, instead of enjoying friendship and intimacy with those around us, we find ourselves fencing with each other, using our talents, achievements, and strengths as weapons. Within our families and friendships, talents and strengths such as attractiveness, intelligence, wit, charm, and artistic and athletic ability, become not what they are intended to be, namely, beautiful gifts and charisms which enrich life, but instead weapons of war, objects of envy, and forces which serve to create jealousy and which alienate us from each other.

Intimacy and love will be achieved only when we stop

our talent parades and give up our propensity for building towers of Babel. Only then, when we are vulnerable and others can see that we and they indeed share a common condition, and that our strengths, talents, and achievements, are not threats, but beautiful gifts which can help enrich their lives; only then will they move towards us in authentic friendship and intimacy. In the movement away from 'alienation-loneliness' one of the first things we must learn to do is to risk a greater vulnerability.

This vulnerability however is not to be confused with weakness. To be vulnerable in the true sense does not mean that someone must become a doormat, a weakling, devoid of all pride, going out of his way to let others know all his faults and weaknesses. Nor is vulnerability to be confused with the idea of 'letting-it-all-hang-out', or any other form of psychological strip-tease. To be vulnerable rather is to be strong enough to present ourselves as we really are with all our strengths and weaknesses, with nothing added and nothing subtracted. To be vulnerable is to be strong enough to be able to present ourselves without false props, without an artificial display of our credentials. In brief, to be vulnerable is to be strong enough to be honest and tender. Like Jesus, the person who is vulnerable is a person who cares enough to let himself be weak, precisely because he does care.

Whenever we find ourselves feeling frustrated by a lack of intimacy within our lives, whenever we feel paranoid and alienated, we should examine ourselves vis-à-vis the question of vulnerability. Perhaps we are not vulnerable enough to be loved.

(3) *Free space*[4]

The movement from 'alienation-loneliness' towards integration also depends upon each of us creating within our relationships a 'free space', a sense of freedom for the other person.

One of the dangers of loneliness, as we saw, is that, because we are so lonely and need affection so desperately, we often tend to become overly possessive and overly demanding within relationships, often virtually suffocating the other with our possessiveness and demands. All of us, I am sure, have experienced both sides of this. For example, all of us have, within those relationships which are dearest to us, experienced a natural inclination to be possessive, to be jealous of the other, to demand from the other an unfair exclusiveness. Conversely, all of us have experienced the someone else's over-possessiveness, his unfair demands for time and exclusiveness, his jealousy, and his 'stickiness' which gives us a feeling of being suffocated.

Hence, we need within our relationships to respect the freedom of the other enough to create for her person a free space: a free space where she may move in or move out; a free space within which she feels loved, but not suffocated; and a free space within which she feels free to grow according to her own inner dictates.

This is probably the hardest thing to create within any friendship. Our hearts spontaneously move out to try to possess that for which they yearn. This creates a problem since, while people enjoy being loved, they do not enjoy being possessed. Perhaps the greatest mark of maturity within relationships is the ability to love someone and yet let her be truly free. That, not sexual performance, is what makes a great lover! An anonymous sage once remarked: 'If you love something, set it free. If it comes back, it is yours, if it doesn't, it never was.' How true and yet how difficult to do!

To create a free space for others is not, however, to be confused with being casual and indifferent within relationships. The space created by coolness, aloofness, and non-attachment is simply an empty space, one which is incapable of being the grounds for love. To let someone be free does not mean that we do not care. We care, and we care greatly! In fact, it is precisely because we do care a great deal that we refuse to violate the other's freedom, regardless of how painful that might be for us.

I once heard a fascinating metaphor for what constitutes a good relationship. A friendship relationship can be compared to two porcupines who got caught in a snowstorm. Whenever they got too far away from each other, they began to feel cold. Yet, they could never get too close to each other without their quills hurting them. Thus, they were forced to maintain a very delicate balance between distance and closeness. Relating within friendship, within family life, and within religious community also requires this same delicate, hard-to-achieve balance. We need to be close, otherwise we feel the cold. Yet we may never be so close that we become over-possessive and begin to suffocate the freedom of the other person.

Moving out of 'alienation-loneliness' is dependent upon our ability to create for others a free space within which they and we can live creatively the tension between closeness and distance.

(4) *Playfulness*[5]

The movement out of alienation is dependent too upon playfulness and humour. By nature we are playful critters. We spontaneously enjoy play, silliness, humour, pranks, and surprises (not to mention wine drinking). It is interesting to note that, while we *admire* smart people and *fear* powerful people, we *like* playful people.

Too often though, we do not build enough playfulness and humour into our relationships. Small wonder we so often get bored with each other! Our relationships are too characterised by seriousness, by the ordinary, by lack of surprise, by lack of playfulness and humour. Very often when we first flirt with each other in friendship, we find each other interesting and exciting. This is because, at this stage, we are playful and silly with each other. Too often, and this is a sad fact, after we get close to each other we stop the playfulness and the silliness and fall rather quickly into a bland dull rut! Why do our marriage partners, our families, our circle of friends, and our religious communities so often appear to us as dull and uninteresting? Often it is because we, and they, have long ago stopped being playful and silly with each other. We have stopped flirting with each other, saving our playfulness only for others. What is needed to constantly renew, rejuvenate, and re-invigorate our relationships is a good bit of flirting, playfulness, humour, and pranks.

For instance, few persons who have seen Neil Simon's *The Goodbye Girl* leave the theatre without envying the relationship that he depicts between two lovers. Why does this relationship strike us as being so attractive? Precisely because it is characterised by much playfulness. For example, at one point in the play, the young man invites his lady friend out to dinner. She returns home from work fully expecting to find him waiting for her, eager to take her to some fancy restaurant. A surprise awaits her. Instead of finding him, she finds a note, directing her to the roof of the apartment building within which she is living. Surprised and confused about what is happening, she proceeds very cautiously to the roof. She peers around in the darkness and is suddenly surprised as her fiancé, dressed as Humphrey Bogart, steps out of a dark corner. The two of them then proceed to spend three of the happiest hours of their lives eating a gourmet meal, in the rain, by candle light, on an apartment roof. Hardly your basic restaurant! But then this is hardly your basic couple!

Love means many things. It means much more than sharing a bed or a building; it means much more than being accidentally thrown together by force of circumstance; and it means much more than merely being bound together by erotic or emotional attraction. It means sharing all things: sorrows and joys, growth and sickness, life and death. It also, if it is to remain alive and interesting, means sharing silliness, playing pranks on each other, and keeping each other alert with wit and surprises.

Whenever the folks gather and some would deign to gripe about alienation, let him who has pulled off a playful prank lately cast the first complaint!

(5) *Crucifixion*[6]

In examining the movement from alienation towards integration we see that it is not easy to create and sustain meaningful contact with each other. In fact, some question whether this is even possible. Can we ever really come together, reach each other, and love each other genuinely, beyond selfishness? Is real human community even possible?

This question does not admit of an easy answer. Today it is not uncommon to be agnostic about the possibility of genuine love. More and more, sensitive persons are despairing of attaining genuine love and declaring that behind all our words and songs of love, there lies only self-interest, selfishness, egoism. Anyone who is sensitive to the pain of our world, and to the pains and movements within his or her own heart, is obliged to ask this question: Is it really possible to come together in true love and intimacy, beyond self-interest and egoism?

Our Christian faith tells us that the answer to that question must be affirmative. Christianity believes in the possibility of human love, in a togetherness which is meaningful, deep, permanent, and beyond self-interest. However, Christianity also affirms that there is a price to be paid for that to become a reality. The price is a radical one, 'crucifixion'. Love cannot be had for a lesser price tag. The example of Christ's own life illustrates this.

I would like to illustrate this by means of an analogy: Ingmar Bergman's movie, *Cries and Whispers*.

In this movie, Bergman asks the question: Is it ever really possible to break through to each other and communicate at a deep level and sustain this? He uses a metaphor to pose and answer this question – the metaphor of touching. He asks through the film: can we ever really touch each other?

He suggests that it can be done, but only if a radical price is paid: a certain 'crucifixion' is needed. His answer affords a rich analogy which can help us to better understand some of Christ's own teaching and example on the question of human community and togetherness.

In *Cries and Whispers* there are four main characters: three sisters, *Agnes, Karin, Maria*, and their maid, *Anna*. Agnes, the eldest sister, gets sick and dies a very painful and ugly death. While she is dying, her two sisters and Anna take care of her. Each of these latter three characters is representative of a certain type of person.

Karin, the second oldest sister, is a very cold, frigid, bitter person. She is unhappily married and has never loved or reached out to anyone.

Maria, the youngest of the sisters, is a very warm and open person. She wants to reach out to people and communicate with them at a deep level. She is, however, unfaithful in her marriage.

Anna, the maid, is presented as faithful and dedicated. She is physically big and clumsy, but very warm, sincere, and responsive.

The story is simple. Agnes gets sick and dies a very painful death. While she is dying, her sisters and Anna take care of her. Her illness is, at times, a very ugly one since it causes her to be disfigured and smelly. Whenever this happens, her sisters, Karin and Maria, always keep a certain 'antiseptic' distance. At these times when her illness makes her unpleasant and smelly, only Anna, the maid, can bring herself to 'touch' her.

The main plot is interspersed with flashbacks to their past life. These flashes show Maria's unfaithfulness to her husband and Karin's unhappy situation with her husband – and how she pathetically wounds herself rather than have him touch her.

The story builds to a climax: Agnes dies. Maria decides to try to use this death as an opportunity to draw closer to her sister, Karin. She approaches Karin, telling her that the death of their sister should be an opportunity for them to come closer to each other. But Karin bitterly lashes out, attacking Maria. Maria persists, however, and eventually breaks through to her sister. They end up 'touching' each other deeply – both physically and otherwise.

At this moment though, Bergman inserts something which (though extremely confusing to the audience at first because it is metaphorical) gives the story a different thrust and an added depth. That is, he has the dead sister, Agnes, call out for the other sisters to come to her, to hold her, and to comfort her dead, decaying body.

Karin goes in first, but soon flees. She tells Agnes that she finds the very idea repulsive. Besides she has never really loved Agnes, or anyone else, to begin with. She runs from the room.

Maria enters next. She moves close to the bed in which Agnes' dead body is lying. She talks to her and slowly moves closer, but always retains her 'antiseptic' distance. Then, in a rather significant scene, Agnes describes to Maria the horror she is experiencing and how she needs Maria to wrap her arms around her and hold her. She asks Maria to draw closer, to take her hand.

Maria edges closer and finally, hesitantly (but none too firmly) places her hand on Agnes' hand. She says to Agnes: 'This is just like when we were kids and stayed out too late and got frightened and cold, and then we would hold each other and we'd feel better.' Agnes now asks her to draw closer still and reaches out and puts her hand on Maria's neck. Maria flees in horror. All her desire to really 'touch' others cannot bring her to pay this price.

After she flees, Anna, the maid, comes in and, in a rather striking scene, we see her sitting on the bed, holding the corpse of Agnes like a mother would hold a child. Her breasts are bared and we get the impression of a mother nursing a child, or a Pietà perhaps.

The next day is the funeral. After the funeral, the family breaks up. Ironically, Anna, the only one who had really loved Agnes, is for all practical purposes rejected by the family. Her giving is not rewarded with gratitude, nor indeed with any financial recompense. She also asks for nothing, to the great relief of the family.

Then, in a final scene, Maria and Karin say goodbye to each other. Karin, who had never experienced real love before her 'touching' incident with Maria, now alludes to that incident. She tells Maria that they have touched each other very deeply. She obviously wants to continue to try to do that.

Maria, however, who ostensibly is the person who wants to reach out and touch people, backs off. She finds that she does not want to sustain that contact. She pretends that she has forgotten about it and says: 'I can't remember every silly little thing I've ever done!' Thus, in a final bit of irony, she makes the incident seem trivial as well.

Ingmar Bergman, in this movie, poses the question: can human beings ever really reach and touch each other in a deep and permanent way?

He suggests an answer – an affirmative answer. However, that answer can be affirmative only if a certain price is paid; namely, are you (metaphorically speaking) willing to go as far as Anna did? Are you willing to hold a corrupting, stinking corpse in your arms and nurse it like a mother would nurse a child? If you cannot do that, then you cannot love fully.

Bergman suggests that there are various degrees and levels here:

Karin, the second oldest sister, is badly scarred as a person and is not even all that interested in trying to reach others. This is the lowest level.

More significant for our purposes is Maria, the youngest of the sisters. She represents most of us. She is a person who very much wants to reach people and 'touch' them. However, despite being able to want all the right things, and say all the right things, and occasionally even do all the right things (for example, when she broke through and reached her sister, Karin), Maria, in the end, failed. She was not able to love others fully. She was not really able to break through to others in a permanent, non-reserved way.

For instance, after breaking through to Karin, she is unable to sustain that relationship and she 'backs off'. Also, unlike Anna, she is unable to really pay the hard price and take that final step, as her encounter with the dead Agnes illustrates. Her remark, 'This is just like when we were kids and stayed out too late and got frightened and cold, and then we would hold each other and we'd feel better', illustrates (for Bergman) precisely where she is at in terms of her reaching out to others, namely, at a kid's level. Despite the fact that, on the surface, she appears to be very open and willing to reach others, she is not able to pay the hard price, like Anna, the maid, was able to do.

Anna is the only one who is really able to touch others and sustain this. Despite the ugliness, smell, and corrupting flesh she could reach out and take another human into her arms. She could relate to people at a deeper level than that of physical and personal attractiveness, cleanliness, natural charm and the like.

She could, in short, cut through the limitedness of the human person and situation, the stench, the sickness, the lack of attractiveness, the weakness, and reach the person who is behind all this, who is limited by it, and who is crying out for someone to reach her very person in a deep, non-reserved, permanent, and unconditional way.

And for this she expects no gratitude or material recompense. She loves simply because people need to be loved! Her love costs her; there is a certain 'crucifixion' on her part.

All of us have a driving need to love. We are made for that; we yearn for it; and we need it. We need to 'touch' others and have them 'touch' us. But the issue is not a simple one. Loving others is simply not all that easy to do! Talking about it, yearning for it, and simply 'doing what comes naturally' is not enough. We have been doing those things; yet, somehow, we have not really made God's kingdom of love and togetherness come. Instead we have all too often been frustrated and dissatisfied in our attempts to reach each other.

What we have missed doing are the hard things, the 'crucifixion' things. We have missed doing a lot of the things that Jesus did: the giving without expecting in return, the forgiving when we are slighted, and the laying down of our lives for others without counting the cost. That is what crucifixion means! Not surprisingly, it is also what real love means.

Unlike Anna, the big clumsy maid of *Cries and Whispers*, we all too frequently do not love people; instead we love certain qualities and charms within them. Thus, we run away from them when they are no longer so naturally attractive to us, but precisely when they really need us the most. Like Maria, we spend a lot of time talking about love, but are unwilling to really give of ourselves or sustain our caring when things get difficult. Our love is much too 'antiseptic'. It is little wonder that the loneliness in our faces decries our many words about love and speaks instead of emptiness and yearning.

Love, as the poets have always said, 'makes the world go round.' It is the most precious and meaningful of all human activities. But it is not, as some would have us believe, an easy thing. We are flawed, weak, grappling, and very *human* beings. For this reason, it is tough business, this learning to love.

Because we are incurably human, love cannot always be 'antiseptic'. We get smelly, sick, and unattractive. We grow older and lose many of our natural charms. Love cannot sustain itself if it is based merely on natural attraction.

In addition, since we are so incredibly human, we do not always appreciate those who love us, nor are we always appreciated by those to whom we give our love. Thus, love cannot always be sustained by warm feelings either.

Love, real love, can be nurtured and sustained only by a certain 'crucifixion' on our part. That is, we can sustain love only by an unconditional and painful giving of ourselves to others, a giving which is not based on mere natural attraction and expectation of gratitude and appreciation. Christ taught us about this type of love. He was crucified so that he might love us. If we can love each other when we are smelly and unattractive, when we are selfish and ungrateful, then we will be sharing in the love that Jesus taught us about.

The answer to much of the loneliness gnawing inside us is togetherness. We have to reach out and touch each other. Human togetherness can take away the painful loneliness from our faces and from our hearts.

But the price of human togetherness is 'crucifixion'. We will find love only to the extent that we can give ourselves like Christ did. For, as a paraphrase of Ephesians 2:13 and 14 would put it, 'It is through crucifixion that the dividing walls between us are knocked down, and we are made one.'

Handling 'restlessness-loneliness': in search of solitude[7]

Even after much of our 'alienation-loneliness' has been overcome, we still suffer from other types of loneliness, particularly 'restlessness-loneliness'. This latter type is perhaps the least recognised and least understood among all the various types of loneliness. It is, as we saw, that loneliness which is present in us precisely because, as persons, we are built for infinite love and unity, and thus are destined to go through this finite life always somewhat restless and dissatisfied. It is also a particularly danger- ous type of loneliness, often either paralysing our creative energies or propelling us outward into frenzied activity.

How is it to be handled creatively? As is the case for all the various types of loneliness, there is no instant solu- tion. Its creative resolution is contingent upon developing certain patterns of living which will bridle its potentially tyrannical forces and turn them into creative energy. How is this to be done? By moving our 'restlessness-loneliness' in the direction of creative solitude.

To do this requires, first of all, that we recognise that this type of loneliness can never be fully overcome in this life. We must begin by accepting the fact that we are pilgrims on earth, destined to be partially restless and unfulfilled, living in a world in which all symphonies remain unfinished. This starting point is crucial because only when we have existentially accepted this fact will we stop letting ourselves be seduced by pseudo solutions. As long as we do not accept that 'restlessness-loneliness' is an incurable part of being human, we will continue to try to find a solution for it in the relentless and frenzied pursuit of experience. We will drink, party, and socialise to the point of exhaustion, but will never put to rest the lonely fires within us. In fact, our pursuit of experience will generally be counterproductive, serving not to still our restlessness, but to fan the flames and intensify the burning. Trying to still 'restlessness-loneliness' by increasing and intensifying social activity is tantamount to throwing fuel on a fire.

However, recognising that 'restlessness-loneliness' can never be fully overcome in this life is not identical with resigning ourselves to stoicism or despair. To a certain extent 'restlessness-loneliness' can be overcome, even in our present condition. However, its resolution, unlike the resolution of 'alienation-loneliness' does not lie in moving outward. It lies in the very opposite direction, in the direction of solitude. To creatively come to grips with 'restlessness-loneliness' each of us must travel *inward*, to meet ourselves, and to meet the infinite love and riches of God dwelling inside of our beings.

How is this journey inward made? It is contingent upon three factors:

(1) *Giving up false messianic expectations*

A sage once remarked: 'The longest journey begins with a single step.' The journey inward towards solitude begins with a single realisation, namely, that there is no full and final solution for loneliness within this life. We are destined to be fully redeemed, and unlonely, only when the kingdom about which Jesus preached comes in all its completeness. In the meantime, we must give up attempting to find complete fulfilment through partial and pseudo solutions. We must face up to our loneliness, accept it, stop running from it, stop letting it propel us into all kinds of dissipating activity, and stop seeing its resolution as lying exclusively in a journey outward. As hard as that is to do, we must, at some point, stop our frenzied activities and look inward for an answer. The journey towards solitude begins with this first step.

It will not be an easy step. Inside of ourselves we are, in many ways, like a parched, thirsty desert. Our hearts and minds, like the desert winds, are hot and restless, relentlessly stirring, pushing us into activity. The pain of stopping our pursuit of activity, and entering alone and in silence into ourselves, is, as we saw, the very experience of purgatory.

(2) *The inward journey*

Once we have stopped running from our loneliness, we must take the next step. Alone, in silence, with all the concomitant pain, we must begin to enter into the parched, thirsty inner depths of our being. This journey, if properly made, will eventually put us into contact with the living waters that Christ promised. It will put us into contact with the infinite riches of infinite love. This, more than any other force, will serve to help still the lonely fires inside us. No amount of external activity can give us this, for what is needed to still the fires of our restlessness for the infinite is a wellspring inside us which draws upon infinite waters.

Concretely, what is to be done? In brief, each of us must enter deeply into ourselves. Especially at those times when we feel our restlessness most acutely we must stop our external activities and be silent and still . . . silent and still long enough that we begin to feel comfortable in silence and stillness. Once we feel comfortable with silence and stillness, we will have begun the journey towards solitude, towards meeting the infinite within our own inner depth. However, as soon as we resume our external activity we will, inevitably (and, most of the time, quickly) lose some or all of the peace we experienced in the stillness. It will be necessary to return to silence. There will be lots of starting over! But, if persevered in, eventually this practice will give us a degree of solitude which will enable us to channel creatively the restless forces inside of us, so we can be at peace with them.

This search for solitude must, however, be sharply distinguished from all unhealthy types of withdrawal. One criterion of discernment which can be used to distinguish a healthy solitude from an unhealthy withdrawal is that healthy solitude leads a person to greater empathy, concern for others, and greater involvement within the world, whereas unhealthy withdrawal leads to greater self-centredness, apathy, and fantasising.

The movement into solitude is best accomplished when the movement into silence is also a movement into explicit prayer. However, prescinding from this ideal, even the simple practice of regularly bringing our external activity to a halt and putting ourselves into quiet and stillness, and staying with the silence until we are comfortable, can be immeasurably helpful in coping with 'restlessness-loneliness'. Prescinding entirely from religious considerations, one of the best ways of coping with the stresses of our hectic age is to spend some time each day in complete silence.

This journey, however, cannot be quickly made. To

enter into solitude requires a great deal of patience and respect. Our heart, and indeed every human heart, is a mystery which may be entered only with reverence. We know that when we interrelate with others we must be careful never to violate their freedom. We must always stand before them patiently, respecting their inner freedom and dictates. When we deal with others, we may encourage, challenge, and perhaps even prod slightly at times, but we may never push too hard. We must respect the mystery that is the human heart. It has, as Pascal aptly put it, its reasons that the head does not know of. Hence there is no place for heavy equipment, heavy words, and ultimatums when dealing with the human heart. The kinks and the knots, the tensions and the hang ups, must be allowed to work themselves out slowly. Great patience and great respect is always required.

This is crucial to remember when we attempt to journey inward towards the depths of our own heart. In the same way as we can violate another person by wading into their subjectivity irresponsibly without the proper respect and reverence, so too, we can violate ourselves, and do ourselves harm, by attempting to wade into our own inner depth without treating our hearts with sufficient respect and patience. Our heart, like everyone else's, is tender and fragile, a mystery to be handled with reverence. It, too, has its kinks and knots, and its reasons which our head does not always understand. Hence, we must have enough patience and respect to back off at times, and let the kinks and knots dissolve themselves according to their own inner dictates. This will be difficult because in our journey inward, as in all else, we want results quickly. We find it hard to wait for the *kairos*, the opportune time. However, as is the case in all authentic human growth, results cannot be forced. There must be sufficient patience to respect the natural rhythms of the organism. There can be no quick shortcuts to solitude.

(3) *A lifelong struggle*

The movement from restlessness to solitude, the journey inward, is never fully achieved, never made once and for all. Solitude is something towards which we move in life, but never attain fully. As Henri Nouwen puts it, 'the world is not divided between lonely people and solitaries.'[8] Rather we go through life fluctuating between the two, different perhaps from hour to hour, week to week, year to year. Sometimes we are more in peaceful solitude, sometimes we are more restless. But within ourselves we can experience a real difference between restless loneliness and peaceful solitude. What is that difference? It is the difference between living in *freedom rather than compulsion; restfulness rather than restlessness; patience rather than impatience; inwardness rather than frenzied outwardness; altruism rather than greediness; authentic friendship rather than possessive clinging; and empathy rather than apathy.*[9]

We know we are moving into solitude when we feel less compulsive and driven, less restless and frenzied, and less greedy and possessive. It is then, too, that we will, for perhaps the first time in our lives, really feel free.

Handling 'fantasy-loneliness': in search of truth[10]

In distinguishing among the various types of loneliness, we saw that one type, 'fantasy-loneliness', is caused by the fact that all of us live out a fantasy of ourselves and our world, a fantasy which is always at least somewhat at variance with reality. How is this type of loneliness to be overcome? By a movement towards a more honest living of truth.

We will become less lonely when we reduce the discrepancy which exists between the fantasies which we have of reality and the real world as it is. How might this discrepancy be reduced? *By prayer.* We move towards a fuller living of reality to the extent that we let prayer offer a critique of our fantasies. Prayer puts us into deeper contact with God, and since God defines reality in its deepest sense, the more we are attuned to His mind, the more we are attuned to reality. Fantasy is broken by prayer. This can best be understood by an analogy. An artefact is most accurately defined by the artist who created it. Accordingly, if we want to fully understand an artefact, we must know somewhat the intention of the artist. The more fully we know the intention of the artist, the more accurately we will understand the artefact. Similarly, if we want to understand reality, we must understand the intention of God, the artist who created this particular artefact. The more fully we know the mind of God, the more accurately we will understand reality. We come to know the mind and intention of God through prayer. Prayer, therefore, is what puts us into contact with the deepest understanding there is of reality. It is prayer that affords us the opportunity to move beyond our fantasies towards truth. Living the truth will make us less lonely.

In one way, therefore, Jesus was the most unalienated person ever in the history of our world. His deep intimacy with His Father prevented any unhealthy fantasies from growing within Him. His long hours in prayer did more than merely put Him into creative solitude, they helped also to dispel slowly all fantasy and untruth from His understanding of Himself and of the world we live in. In prayer, Jesus not only got to know the Father, but, as He got to know Him, He also got to know Himself and the world. Eventually He knew the truth. It is ironic that He remained silent when Pontius Pilate questioned Him concerning the meaning of truth.

Prayer is the path out of our alienating fantasies. However, the type of prayer which leads us to deeper truth may not be simply identified with formal prayer, namely, explicit discursive prayer, meditation, contemplation, the Jesus Prayer, the rosary, and various forms of liturgical prayer. These will clearly play a large role in helping bring us to the truth. But, prayer also has a much wider sense. God speaks to us everywhere. We are praying, too, when we read and study Scripture, when we study our Christian roots, when we study the opinions of wise persons throughout history, when we listen to the opinions of those around us, when we read God's language in the secular events of our world, and when we listen to the authentic wisdom of science and the arts. We must let God, speaking through all these, challenge us out of our fantasies and illusions. When we listen to God in prayer much of the loneliness from which we suffer because of our fantasies and illusions will dissolve.

This movement, from 'fantasy-loneliness' to a truer living of reality, is, like all the other movements out of loneliness, a lifelong task. There are no overnight formulae, only long hours, days and years, of patience and struggle. Hopefully as we grow older we will grow wiser and less lonely as we let prayer slowly dissolve our fantasies into reality.

Handling 'rootlessness-loneliness': in search of the stillpoint

'Home is where one starts from,' said T. S. Eliot. However, moving away from home, especially if we do it frequently, can also be the cause of much loneliness. All of us experience, to a greater or lesser extent, a loneliness which results from not having enough anchors, enough absolutes, and enough permanent roots to make us feel secure and stable in a world which is characterised by transience. As we saw when we differentiated among the various types of loneliness, there is prevalent today in our world and inside ourselves, a certain 'rootlessness-loneliness'.

How is this type of loneliness to be overcome? Its resolution, like the resolution of the other types of loneliness, lies in a lifelong movement towards a certain goal. However, in this case, the goal is not so much one of increased integration, increased solitude, or increased prayer, though these factors will play a part. Rather the goal is that of finding for ourselves certain stillpoints, clefts in the rock, so to speak, which will help give us a sense of security in a world which is too frequently shifting. This security will make us less lonely. But where and how do we find these stillpoints?

Here I would like to suggest *five* complementary approaches which we might use to help us find and create certain stillpoints within our lives. Some are specifically theological, others are not. All, hopefully, can be useful in helping us overcome the nagging rootlessness which so often makes us lonely.

(1) *A movement towards that which is beyond time*

All that is within time is impermanent, shifting, changing, and ultimately destined to vanish. To find something upon which we can ultimately anchor ourselves, we must then search for those things which are, somehow, beyond the parameters of time and history. This moves us into the realm of faith. It is faith which can put us into contact with cults and creeds, moral codes and principles, which, prescinding from their concrete embodiment in symbol and language, are ultimately beyond the transient. These can put us into contact with that which does not shift, namely, the person of infinite love and fidelity, the God who is the Father of Jesus, the Yahweh who spoke His word to Israel, and the timeless, eternal, ever old yet ever new God who has been the great stillpoint for millions of persons who could not even pronounce His name.

There is an ultimate anchor. There is a great stillpoint. There is something beyond transience, beyond time and history, beyond the shifting, relative, unfirm, and non-permanent world we live in. There is something that cannot be razed to the ground by progress, debunked by critical investigation, or rendered obsolete by new

discoveries. That something is a Someone. That Someone is contacted by journeying into the realms of faith,
hope, and selflessness. A journey into this realm, if persevered in, will help dispel much of our lonely rootlessness.

(2) Commitment

Much of our 'rootlessness-loneliness' can be overcome by
committing ourselves to certain persons, values, things,
and projects, and then refusing to be unfaithful to those
commitments. Much of our rootlessness is caused by lack
of commitment and infidelity. Our lives are too much
characterised by our refusal to commit ourselves per-
manently to anything, whether it be another person, a
religious community, or even just a certain job, a certain
neighbourhood, or a certain set of values. We all want to
'hang loose'! As well, and tragically so, our lives are too
characterised by infidelity, by broken promises, broken
words, cheap commitments, and hastily withdrawn loyal-
ties. It is not surprising that we suffer from an acute
loneliness.

What is needed to combat 'rootlessness-loneliness' is
commitment and fidelity. We must relearn what the word
permanence adds to the words *love, commitment,
friendship, promise, vow*, and *loyalty*. Only then will we
again discover, right within these things, something
which is beyond time. As long as we continue to prefer
trial marriage to real commitment, temporary religious
affiliation to final vows, and freedom to go back on our
promises to viewing our given word as sacred, we should
not be so surprised if our lives are haunted by a gnawing
rootlessness.

Thomas More once remarked: 'When a man gives his
word, when he takes an oath or makes a promise, he holds
himself like water, cupped in the palm of his own hand. If
he should be unfaithful then, if he should open his hand,
his integrity pours out. He can never hope to recapture
himself again.'[11] Whenever we cut our roots through

infidelity, through empty words, broken promises, and disloyalty, we should not be surprised that we find it hard to anchor ourselves again.

Pierre Teilhard de Chardin, the philosopher-scientist, experienced during his life much frustration with his own religious family. Misunderstood and at times openly persecuted, he was occasionally encouraged by his friends and colleagues to abandon his commitment to his religious family. Teilhard, however, would always dismiss this with the simple statement: 'I can never leave because *I have given my word!*'

(3) *Renewing our sense of history*

Today there is a renewed interest in history, at all levels. Historians are refining their methods and are showing enthusiastic interest in ancient documents; archaeologists are looking for new digs; biblical scholars are hunting for newer caves which might contain older writings; religious congregations are trying to rediscover the spirit of their founders; and ethnic groups are searching for their roots. All this is a healthy sign.

No matter who we are, we stand within a rich tradition and history. We need to develop a sense of tradition and history, and of our place in it. An understanding of this can give us more stability, more roots, which can help us to anchor ourselves within the shifting winds of our times. The movement out of 'rootlessness-loneliness' is partly contingent upon a sense of history and tradition.

(4) *Slow down the input*[12]

Part of our 'rootlessness-loneliness' is caused by future shock, namely, by the pace at which people, organisations, knowledge, places, and things move through our lives. Accordingly part of the solution to this problem lies precisely in the movement towards slowing down and ordering the intake of these. We simply have to make a conscious effort to have persons, organisations, knowledge, places, and things pass through our life more slowly, or at least at a pace which we can more easily accept. We must, at times, lower the level of stimulation and novelty.

To accomplish this effectively we must be extremely concrete and practical. For example, to suggest just a few things: we should avoid moving unnecessarily, keep more contact with our family and former friends, write more letters, listen to less sound, look at less bright lights, have more escape hatches, play more, read more detective novels, take more walks by ourselves, and use fewer throwaway items. We should stop buying a new car each year, and instead, buy one, give it a name, become attached to it, and drive it until it won't drive anymore! We should stop buying ball-point pens and buy ourselves a fountain pen – and become unhealthily attached to it! By doing these things we will be slowing down the input of novelty and stimulation, retaining more constants within our lives, and, in some small degree becoming less lonely.

(5) *Conscious response*

Albert Einstein once remarked: 'Experience is not what happens to you, but what you do with what happens to you.' In combating 'rootlessness-loneliness' it is important that we act reflectively. It is important that we consciously try to control life and circumstance, rather than let it control us. To do this, it is necessary for us to consciously work at controlling circumstance, and at positively creating stability zones within our lives. Again, a few suggestions will help illustrate this:

(i) *Plan your life to a certain degree*

Make a budget of how you will spend your emotional and physical energies. Set priorities and try to stick to them. Do not leave all to chance and circumstance, preferring to do what comes naturally. What comes naturally is a flurry of ever-increasing activity which leaves us dissipated, lonely and frustrated.

(ii) *Have and develop ritual*

Ritual links us to the past and helps to give us certain stability zones. For example, celebrate anniversaries, birthdays, and holidays. Ritually revisit places and ritually redo certain things which were particularly meaningful to you. Make certain things, for example: the World Series, the Super Bowl, the Academy Awards, and so on, into ritual family events. All of these, prescinding entirely from their particular interest to us, can potentially provide us with opportunity for ritual.

(iii) *Write*[13]

Keep a diary or a journal. Write down your feelings and reflections. Few things can be as profitable to help us reflect creatively upon our lives as is writing.

Home is, indeed, where we start from! We will suffer much loneliness on the journey from our first home to our last one. But, as we travel from that first home to our final home, to the degree that we find and create certain still-points for ourselves, we will be less lonely along the road.

Handling 'blues-loneliness': in search of an ad hoc solution

In distinguishing among the various types of loneliness, we saw that one type, 'blues-loneliness', is more or less identical with psychological and physical depression. It is a type of loneliness which is generally ephemeral and is triggered by a very specific cause, for example, the death of a loved one, excessive physical or emotional fatigue, menopause, physical illness, psychological illness, or a dreary rainy day. This type of loneliness has less of a theological dimension to it than do the other types. While it is an important and painful type of loneliness, impossible to ignore, creative suggestions regarding its resolution should come more from the realms of psychiatry, psychology, medicine, and common sense, rather than from any specifically theological discipline. Hence little will be said here.

Unlike the other forms of loneliness which can be handled creatively only by moving in a certain clearly defined direction, 'blues-loneliness' must be handled more on an ad hoc basis. It is impossible to formulate a spirituality of the blues since its causes are so diverse.

Creative resolution of 'blues-loneliness' lies in a great variety of things, depending, of course, on what is causing our 'blues'. Sometimes what is required is simply patience, given time the pain will pass. Or, perhaps we might need a holiday, or medical, psychiatric, or psychological help. Maybe we need to read books which will give us a deeper self-understanding; or perhaps we just need a good hot bath, or a night out, or the company of a friend. The 'blues' are caused by many things. Accordingly there are many approaches needed to handle them creatively.

Towards a final solution: in search of the community of life

In our analysis of human loneliness we saw that according to a Christian understanding of it, loneliness can only be partially resolved while we are here on earth. While here we are merely pilgrims, journeying towards that which can fulfil the infinite caverns of our hearts and minds, namely, an all-in-one-flesh community of life with God and each other. Only when we are fully part of this community of life will we be fully unlonely.

However, this togetherness in a community of life is already partially a reality. As members of the body of Christ we are already in that community. Through faith and hope we are already in community of life with God, and through charity we are already in community of life with each other. To the extent that we are already participating in this community of life, we are already moving towards and achieving the final solution for our loneliness.

For the Christian this points to the importance not only of a life of faith and charity, but also to the importance of explicit Church membership, especially to the importance of gathering with each other, in community, around God's word and His banquet table. It is here, when we are gathered with each other around God's word and table, that we begin in a radical way to build that all-in-one-flesh unity which will take all our loneliness away.

Jesus had precisely our loneliness in mind when, on the night before He died, He called His followers around a table. It was here that He gave us the possibility of a final solution to our loneliness:

IT WAS A COLD, DARK THURSDAY NIGHT.
A man was discouraged,
Discouraged as only one could be,
Who looks on much hard work,
on much sincerity,
and sees only failure,
and a sinking sun.

ON THAT DARK THURSDAY NIGHT,
A man feels alone,
and lonely,
and frightened.
He sweats blood, in darkness,
the blood of loneliness,
the loneliness of all people.

ON THAT DARK THURSDAY NIGHT,
A man looked on loneliness, and
He yearned to heal.

He yearned to lead all into unity,
Into Community, and
Out of the damned aloneness
Which keeps people from warmth and life.

ON THAT DARK THURSDAY NIGHT,
A man sweats blood,
in body and spirit.
He sweats in darkness,
He sweats in loneliness,
And
it is then . . .

ON THAT DARK THURSDAY NIGHT, THAT
A man takes bread and wine, and says:
'This is my body, this is my blood,
Meet often,
Eat this bread, drink this wine,
And when you do,
I'll be there, and . . .

AS ON THIS DARK THURSDAY NIGHT,
I'll be leading you out of fear and loneliness,
Out of isolation and darkness,
Into Communion,
Into a community of warmth and life,
with God, and
with each other.'

ON ONE DARK THURSDAY NIGHT,
When the sun had long gone down,
And hope and warmth had said good-bye,
When the darkness of loneliness had seemed to win the
    earth,
We were given,
as a gift from God,
the possibility of Community.

NOTES

Chapter 1

1. For detailed statistics see: *Annual Abstract of Statistics*, Central Statistical Office, HMSO, or: *Social Trends*, Central Statistical Office, HMSO.

2. For some examples, see the selected bibliography.

3. Carl Rogers, *On Becoming a Person, A Therapist's View of Psychotherapy*, Boston, Houghton Mifflin Company, c1961, p. 26.

Chapter 2

1. Joseph L. Hart, in a book entitled, *Loneliness: Issues of Emotional Living in an Age of Stress, for Clergy and Religious*, has an extremely good article on 'Perils of the Pleaser'.

Hart points out that 'pleasers' usually end up suffering from *seven* problems:

GUILT – because they cannot please all of the people, all of the time; CONFORMITY – at the expense of self-determination; OVERRELIANCE ON PRAISE – for motivation and to make their life meaningful; DEPRESSION – when praise is absent or criticism is present; INABILITY TO ACCEPT A COMPLIMENT – since they are 'pleasers', and hand out compliments cheaply they find it hard to accept the sincerity of others' compliments; LOSS OF SELF-IDENTITY – they try to please so badly that they play any role which they feel will please others, often never finding out what role would be their true one; NEED TO WEAR MASKS – in order to please they must often hide their own feelings and pretend to feel things in a way that will please others.

(*Loneliness, Issues of Emotional Living in an Age of Stress for Clergy and Religious*, Edited by James P. Madden, Whitinsville, Massachusetts, Affirmation Books, c1977, pp. 41–46.)

2. Gregory of Nyssa: on Virginity; PG. 46, 352 AD, cited in: *From Glory to Glory*, Edited by Jean Danielou and H. Musurillo, Charles Scribner's Sons, New York, N.Y. 1961, pp. 102–103.

3. John Updike, *Rabbit Run*, London, André Deutsch, 1972.

4. Catherine de Hueck Doherty, *Poustinia*, Notre Dame, Ind., Ave Maria Press, 1975, p. 23.

5. For some excellent illustrations of this see: Judith Rossner's *Looking for Mr. Goodbar* (N.Y., Pocket Books, 1976.) Also see the movie *Rachel, Rachel*.

6. Margaret Laurence, *The Stone Angel*, Toronto, McClelland and Stewart Limited, 1968.

Also, to see similar illustrations of how loneliness can harden a person, if it is not faced, see: François Mauriac, *Woman of the Pharisees*, N.Y., Noonday Press, 1946, and, Brian Moore, *The Lonely Passion of Judith Hearne*, Toronto, Little, Brown and Company, c1955.

7. Laurence, *op. cit.*, p. 133.

8. Laurence, *op. cit.*, p. 129.

9. Laurence, *op. cit.*, p. 292.

10. Laurence, *op. cit.*, p. 4.

11. John of the Cross, *The Ascent of Mount Carmel*, Book I, Chapters 6–10. (For a good English translation see: Kieran Kavanaugh, *The Collected Works of St. John of the Cross*, Washington, D.C., ICS Publications Institute of Carmelite Studies, 1973.)

Chapter 3

1. A word of apology for this section. I am aware that much of what I will say in this section will be oversimplified and lack proper nuance. Also, I am aware too that even the very word 'Humanism' is problematic in theology since one may not so easily divide, with total validity, people into two groups: 'Christians' and 'Humanists' – as one might divide sheep from goats.

However, despite these shortcomings, I feel that these generalisations, as most generalisations, nonetheless serve a useful
purpose in that they help us to differentiate among vast
amounts of matter by using relatively simple, though carica-
tured, pictures. What is important in using generalisations
of this kind is to admit them precisely as generalisations, ideal
types, with all the limitations that this implies. It is also
important to attempt to present them in a way that does not
deliberately caricature or distort them. My bold hope is that, in
this section, I will be sensitive on both counts.

2. This idea, explicit in the writings of K. Marx and L.
Feuerbach, is implicit (and often unrecognised) in the thought of
many persons in our society today; e.g., How many persons,
when all is said and done, really do not believe that religion is
somehow impoverishing of what is truly human and creative
within the human person? Why, for example, do so many of the
educated, creative, and talented persons in our society feel the
need to jettison their religious beliefs?

3. Gail Sheehy, *Passages, Predictable Crises of Adult Life*,
Toronto, Bantam Books, 1977 (See p. 252 for just one example of
her claim to be *descriptive*, not *prescriptive*.)

4. John Steinbeck, *The Grapes of Wrath*, Bantam Books, The
Viking Press, N.Y., 1966. pp. 37 & 38.

5. See for example: Rachel Carson, *Silent Spring*, N.Y.,
Fawcett Crest Books. Also, Loren Eiseley, *The Immense
Journey*, N.Y., Random House, 1957.

6. Albert Camus, *The Fall*, Translated by Justin O'Brien,
New York, N.Y. Alfred A. Knopf, Inc. 1973, pp. 80–81.

7. See bibliography. (I would especially recommend Nouwen,
Dunne, Heagle, and Lauder.)

8. In stressing the importance of this point, I am reminded
of a distinction made by Belgian theologian, Norbert Max
Wildiers. He makes a distinction between what he terms a
'theologian' and what he terms a 'religious thinker'. For him,
a 'religious thinker' is one who begins by asking and living a
question. A 'theologian', on the other hand, is one who begins
with an *answer*, and then tries to find a question to fit that
answer. (Lecture given at Newman Theological College,
Edmonton, Alberta, 1976).

9. For example see: Gustavo Gutierrez, *A Theology of
Liberation*, Maryknoll, N.Y., Orbis Books, 1973.

Chapter 4

1. Rubin Gotesky, 'Aloneness, Loneliness, Isolation, Solitude,' in *An Invitation to Phenomenology*, James Edie, General Editor, Chicago, Quadrangle Books, 1965, pp. 211–240.
2. Others who offer useful categories include:
Clarke Moustakas, *Loneliness*, N.J., Prentice-Hall, 1961, and his more recent book: *Loneliness and Love*, N.J., Prentice-Hall, 1972.
William Sadler, 'On the Verge of a Lonely Life', in *Humanitas*, Vol. 10, 1974, pp. 225–277.
William J. Byron, *Alienation: Plight of Modern Man*, (William Bier, General Editor) N.Y., Fordham University Press, 1972, pp. 263ff.
3. In developing my own set of categories, I am indebted to Henri Nouwen's excellent book, *Reaching Out*, (N.Y., Doubleday, 1975). This was helpful to me in developing the idea of 'fantasy-loneliness'. However, my ideas on this point are not always and everywhere identical to his.
4. St Augustine, *Confessions*, Book I, Chapter I.
Also, for this paragraph, I am indebted to John Heagle, *Life to the Full*, Thomas More Press, Chicago, 1976. (Chapter 2.)
5. Edwin Arlington Robinson, 'Richard Cory'.
On this point see also an excellent article by James Carroll, 'Hoping Sun, Sunny Hope', in *National Catholic Reporter*, March 5, 1976.
6. Albert Camus, *The Fall*, N.Y., Knopf, 1973, p. 30.
7. St Augustine, *Confessions*, Book I, Chapter I.
8. Qoheleth 3, 11. This is my own paraphrase of the text – based upon the majority opinion among scripture scholars today. For example see: Christian Ginsburg, *The Song of Songs and Qoheleth*, N.Y.
9. Letter from a former retreatant. (Emphases are my own.)
10. Joseph Marechal, *Studies in the Psychology of Mystics*, N.Y., Magi Books, 1964, pp. 100–101.
11. Ingmar Bergman, Letter in *San Francisco Chronicle*, Sunday, October 5, 1975, p. 15.
12. Richard Bach, *Jonathan Livingston Seagull*, London, Pan Books, 1973.
13. Kazimierz Dabrowski, *Psychoneurosis Is not an Illness*, London, Gryf Publications Ltd., 1972.

14. See: Thomas Aquinas, *De Veritate*, for its classic expression. Also see any standard scholastic textbook on epistemology.

15. Ralph McInerny, *Gate of Heaven*, San Francisco, Harper and Row, 1975, pp. 44–47.

16. Luke 9:58 and parallels.

17. The phenomenon created by Alex Haley's *Roots* is indicative of our thirst precisely for these types of anchors.

18. Mary Lukas and Ellen Lukas, *Teilhard, The Man, The Priest, The Scientist*, N.Y., Doubleday and Company, 1977, pp. 23ff.

19. Alvin Toffler, *Future Shock*, N.Y., Bantam Books, 1970, p. 56.

20. Carole King, from the album *Tapestry*.

Chapter 5

1. For an analysis of sin as a cause for loneliness see:
Richard Wolff, *The Meaning of Loneliness*, Wheaton, Illinois, 60187, Key Publishers, 1970, pp. 47–67.
Yvonne Sell, 'Moving Towards God and Others,' in *Our Family* Feb., 1978, pp. 4–8.

2. For some interesting reflections on the Cain and Abel story see:
Elie Wiesel, *Messengers of God: Biblical Portraits and Legends*, N.Y., Random House, 1976, pp. 37–64.

3. Genesis 2:25.

4. Genesis 3:7.

5. Genesis 11:1–9.

6. See, for example, scriptural commentaries on Acts 2:1–13. (e.g., the commentary of Richard Dillon and Joseph Fitzmyer, in *The Jerome Biblical Commentary*.)

7. For examples see:
Robert Gordis, *Koheleth – The Man and His World*, N.Y., Block Publishing Co., c1955.
Addison Wright, 'The Riddle of the Sphinx: The Structure of the Book of Qoheleth,' in *Catholic Biblical Quarterly*, Vol. 30, 1968, pp. 313–334.

8. Qoheleth 2:11, 17, 26; 4:4, 16; 6:9.

9. Qoheleth 1:2–11. (Revised Standard Version)

10. Qoheleth 6:7. (Revised Standard Version)

11. This word (ha olam) 'Timeliness' has caused more than a few disputes among scholars. There is much difficulty vis-à-vis its translation and its interpretation. However, the majority of scholars, even if they do not translate it as 'timelessness,' agree that it contains that idea. (See, for example, the work of Christian D. Ginsbury, *The Song of Songs and Qoheleth*, N.Y., Ttay Publishing, 1970) Ginsburg did an extensive study of the history of the interpretation of this verse (including Jewish and Rabbinical interpretations) and he concluded that the minority opinions were forced and artificial – both in terms of linguistics and interpretation.

12. Psalm 63. (Jerusalem Bible)

13. Psalm 42–43 (Jerusalem Bible)

14. Psalm 81, Job 23.

15. This motif is present in the entire second half of the Book of Qoheleth. As well, it is already present, as a minor motif, in the first half of the book; e.g., Qoheleth 2:24; 3:12; 3:22; 5:18–19; 7:14; 9:7–10; 11:8–0.

16. Actually Qoheleth sees this brand of Stoicism as the solution to all kinds of loneliness. This, however, was largely due to the fact that he, himself, did not seemingly believe in any worthwhile life after death (Qoheleth 9:10). Hence everything had to somehow be settled satisfactorily in this life. This view, though, is only partially true for the rest of the Old Testament.

17. The whole Book of Job is paradigmatic of this. As well, this message is seen frequently in the teachings of the prophets.

18. Isaiah 11:2–10; Joel 2:28ff., Isaiah 25:6–10 give rich images of this. Also, looking at the Old Testament and how it sees loneliness, we notice that its views are quite finely varied. It makes a distinction between the different kinds of loneliness. Without straining for analogies we see that some comparison to our ideal types of loneliness can be profitably made:

– The type of loneliness which is caused by sin is largely 'alienation-loneliness'. Also, sin is partially responsible for 'fantasy-loneliness'. These types of loneliness, in the Old Testament, are never considered to be healthy. They are always indicative of the fact that something is amiss. Furthermore, the Old Testament sees these two types of loneliness as capable of being, for the most part, overcome in this present life, depending of course on our willingness and ability to convert and move away from selfishness.

– The type of loneliness caused by the structure of human nature (with its inbuilt timelessness and thirst for God) is 'restlessness-loneliness'. In dealing with this type of loneliness, it is significant to note that the Old Testament sees no full human solution to the problem. No amount of human friendship, success, or experience can ever fully fill this gap. It can only be partially overcome in this life. The solution to it lies in prayer and growth into the faith community.

– The loneliness caused by the transitory character of all things created is obviously similar to 'rootlessness-loneliness'. The solution here lies in living a correct relationship to the persons and events of our life.

– 'Fantasy-loneliness' is seen as being partly caused by sin, and partly caused by our failure to live properly our trust relationship to God, others, and the world. It is significant to note that very often our failure to recognise, understand, and accept 'restlessness-loneliness' results in the intensification of 'fantasy-loneliness'.

Chapter 6

1. Romans 14:17
2. Thomas Wolfe, 'God's Lonely Man', in *The Hills Beyond*, N.Y., Signet Classic, 1968, pp. 152–153.
3. Romans 24:32.
4. Mt. 25:1–13. The parable of the ten virgins teaches this. The five foolish virgins, precisely, forgot that they were pilgrims on earth.
5. Hebrews 13:14.
6. For an excellent analysis of how the 'kingdom' has a double dimension to it, i.e., an 'already' and 'not yet', see:
Rudolf Schnackenburg, *God's Rule and Kingdom*, Montreal, Palm Publishers, 1963.
Hans Küng, 'God's Kingdom', in *On Being a Christian*, Collins, London, 1977, pp. 215–226.
7. Alvin Toffler, *Future Shock*, N.Y., Bantam Books, 1970, p. 14.
8. The historical Jesus' own understanding (consciousness) of this in all its exactness is a point of debate within Christology. However, certainly a fair amount is clear by the time the last

New Testament book was written. (See, for example, Reginald H. Fuller's *The Foundations of New Testament Christology*, N.Y., Charles Scribner's Sons, 1965, for an excellent discussion of this.)

9. This aspect of 'realised eschatology' is too frequently neglected within our theologies. Yet, the New Testament unequivocally affirms its importance. St Paul, for instance, in describing baptism, sees us as having *already* risen from the dead (Col. 2). As well, in his theology of the Body of Christ (1 Corinthians and elsewhere) he sees us as *already* being vitally and 'quasi-organically' united within a body. (See: John A. T. Robinson, *The Body, A Study in Pauline Theology*, SCM Press, London, 1966.)

10. Henri Nouwen, *Out of Solitude*, Notre Dame, Indiana, Ave Maria Press, 1974, pp. 51–53 gives an excellent description of what this interim eschatological age means.

11. For one of the more interesting descriptions of heaven, see: Andrew Greeley, *Life for a Wanderer*, N.Y., Doubleday, 1969, pp. 155–165.

12. Mark 1:15.

13. An apologetic footnote is in order here: obviously, here, Jesus is referring to more than just the question of human loneliness. However, the burden would weigh heavily on the person who would try to prove that He was not at all referring to loneliness.

14. Mt. 5:7 and parallels.

15. Mt. 25:31–46.

16. Mt. 25:1–13.

17. Mt. 1:23; 7:11–12; 18:19–20; 28:18–20; John 15:7–17.

Also, for some expatiation on what implications flow from the fact that we, as members of the Body of Christ, are part of God's incarnate presence – see: Jerome Murphy O'Connor, *Becoming Human Together*, Wilmington, Delaware, Michael Glazier Inc. 1977 and: Jerome Murphy O'Connor, 'Prayer of Petition and Community', in *What is Religious Life?* St Saviour's, Dublin, Dominican Publications, pp. 31–52.

18. John 6.

19. Mt. 8:27ff.

20. How is this possible? Are not a sustained self-identity and an all-embracing unity mutually exclusive? The experience of being loved within a community, as well as the findings of

modern sociology and psychology, tell us that, opposing these
two is an illicit dichotomy. Paradoxically, unity and embrace
heighten self-identity rather than diminish it.

21. Again an apologetic footnote is in order. By this, I do not
want to imply that non-believers cannot be saved.

22. Unlike Gnosticism, past and present, which makes revelation and salvation contingent upon certain things mysterious, or certain things not accessible to all, Jesus' message is
open to all, open for public examination.

23. Mt. 5:8.

24. Rev. 22:17.

25. Translation is my own.

26. For example: Exodus 33:18–23.

27. Job 23; Psalm 42; Psalm 62; Psalm 83.

28. Mt. 5:8.

29. Ingmar Bergman, 'Through a Glass Darkly', in *Three
Films by Ingmar Bergman*, translated by Paul Britten Austin,
N.Y., Grove Press Inc., 1970, pp. 15–61.

30. See Footnote 11, Chapter 4.

31. Not a direct quote (I do not have the actual text) but a
fairly close paraphrase.

32. Again, without straining for similarities we see that an
easy and important co-relation can be made between the New
Testament's analysis of loneliness and the ideal types which
were outlined in Chapter 4. That is:

– Sin is what is largely responsible for 'alienation-loneliness'.
It is also responsible for some 'fantasy-loneliness'.

– Our status as pilgrims on earth and our anthropological
make-up is what is responsible for 'restlessness-loneliness', and
for some 'rootlessness-loneliness'.

In the New Testament, the answer for all types of loneliness,
as outlined in this chapter, is conversion and movement into the
faith community.

Chapter 7

1. Willa Cather. Quoted by Gail Sheehy, in *Passages*,
Toronto, Bantam Books, 1977. p. 28.

2. St Augustine, *Confessions*, Book I, Chapter 1.

3. St Augustine, *De Trin.* XIII, 5, 8; *De Genesi Contra*

Manichaeos, i, 20,31; *De Libro Arbitrio* ii, 13, 35–36; and *De Moribus Ecclesiae* i, 25,47.

4. Blaise Pascal, *Pensées*, Baltimore, Penguin Books, 1966, No. 136, p. 67.

5. For a good exposition of Augustine's Neo-platonic background, see: W. T. Jones, *The Medieval Mind, A History of Western Philosophy*, San Francisco, Harcourt, Brace and World, Inc., 1960.

6. See: F. J. Sheed, *Our Hearts Are Restless: The Prayer of St Augustine*, N.Y., Seabury Press, 1976.

7. Actually these points are already present (implicitly) in Augustine's anthropology. What Thomas does essentially is give them a more explicit expression.

8. See: Thomas Aquinas,

Summa Contra Gentiles: II, 21
   II, 55
   III, 25ff.
   III, 69–70

Summa Theologica: I.q.I,a.7
   I.q.12
   I.q.22,a.1
   I.q.75,a.6
   I.q.83,a.1–3
   I.q. 103,a.1
   I/II q.2,a.8
   I/II q.3,a.8
   I/II q.4,a.6
   II/II
   q.17,a.2

9. J. F. Donceel, *Philosophical Anthropology*, N.Y., Sheed and Ward, 1967, pp. 314–371.

10. See, for example, L. Vander Kerken, *Loneliness and Love*, N.Y., Sheed and Ward, 1967.

11. John of the Cross, *The Living Flame of Love*, Commentary on Stanza 3, No. 18. (For a translation see: Kieran Kavanaugh and Otilio Rodriguez, *The Collected Works of St John of the Cross*, Washington, D.C., ICS Publications, Institute of Carmelite Studies, 1973, p. 617ff.)

12. For John of the Cross, the word 'memory' means roughly what we today would connote by our term 'personality' – or, what in process thought, following Whitehead, would be termed our 'consequent nature'.

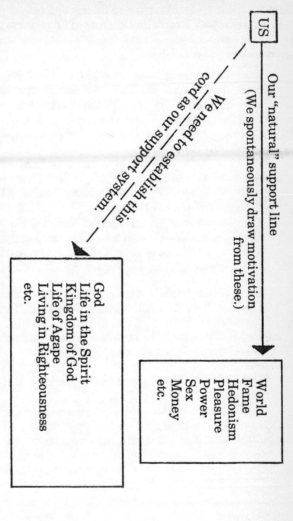

US

Our "natural" support line
(We spontaneously draw motivation
from these.)

We need to establish this
cord as our support system.

World
Fame
Hedonism
Pleasure
Power
Sex
Money
etc.

God
Life in the Spirit
Kingdom of God
Life of Agape
Living in Righteousness
etc.

The shift from one support-system to the other is the pain of purgatory.

13. John of the Cross, *The Ascent of Mount Carmel*, Book I, Chapters 6–10. (Kavanaugh and Rodriguez, *op. cit.*, pp. 84–95.)

14. See Chapter 2 on 'The Dangers of Loneliness'.

15. For John of the Cross there are three stages to our experience of these caverns:

(i) *Stage before religious sensibility:* We have very little religious desire and we feel our loneliness less because we have blunted it by sin. (Reference here is primarily to 'restlessness-loneliness' and 'fantasy-loneliness'.)

(ii) *After a period of purification:* We experience a blinding, raging thirst (terribly painful). Why? Because we have shifted away from the world – but have not yet filled our caverns with the infinite. We are in the process of shifting life-support lines, of severing one umbilical cord and attaching ourselves to another.

(iii) *Contemplation:* Experience of 'Infused Contemplation' (Realised Eschatology) begins to fill in our lonely caverns.
See: *The Living Flame of Love*, Commentary on Stanza 3, No. 18–25. (Kavanaugh and Rodriguez, *op. cit.*, pp. 617ff.)

16. For a fuller explanation see Rahner's articles in *Sacramentum Mundi* on: 'Beatific Vision', 'Freedom', 'Grace', 'Man', 'Order', 'Parousia', 'Person', 'Potentia Obedientialis'.

17. Karl Rahner and Herbert Vorgrimler, *Theological Dictionary*, Freiburg, Verlag, Herder, 1965, p. 367.

18. *Idem.*

19. Karl Rahner, *Theological Investigations*, Vol. IV, Baltimore, Helicon Press, 1966, p. 184.

20. This distinction between *explicit* and *implicit* knowledge should in no way be confused with the psychological distinction between the *conscious* and the *sub-* or *unconscious*. Rahner's distinction is not a psychological one but a philosophical one. This is important to note since, for him, implicit knowledge is (or at least can be) conscious knowledge.

Chapter 8

1. Dag Hammarskjold, *Markings*, translated by Leif Sjoberg and W. H. Auden, London, Faber and Faber, 1964, p. 85.

2. Karl Jaspers, *The Way to Wisdom*, New Haven, Yale University Press, 1964, p. 20.

3. Hammarskjold, *op. cit.*, p. 169.

4. For a fine explanation of this, see: Henri Nouwen, *Out of Solitude*, Notre Dame, Ave Maria Press, 1974, pp. 35–37.

5. Soren Kierkegaard, The first *Diapsalmata*, which stands at the beginning of *Either/Or* (quoted by Walter Lawrie, *Kierkegaard*, Volume I, N.Y., Harper and Row (1962, p. 1.).

6. Colleen McCullough, *The Thorn Birds*, N.Y., Harper and Row, opening page.

7. John of the Cross, *The Living Flame of Love*, Commentary on Stanza 2, No. 17 (Kavanaugh and Rodriguez, *op. cit.*, p. 601).

8. I heartily recommend the following:

Eugene Kennedy, *Living with Loneliness*, Chicago, Thomas More Press, 1973.
Henri Nouwen, *Out of Solitude*, Notre Dame, Ind., Ave Maria Press, 1974.
——, *Reaching Out*, Doubleday, 1975.
——, *The Wounded Healer*, Doubleday, 1972.
Clark Moustakas, *Loneliness and Love*, N.J., Prentice-Hall Inc., 1972.

9. Henri Nouwen, 'Listen to Pain With Heart', in *National Catholic Reporter*, Sept. 6, 1974, p. 15.

10. Robert Frost, 'Mending Wall', in *Great Poems of the English Language*, Compiled by Wallace Alvin Briggs, N.Y., Tudor Pub. Co., 1933, p. 1257.

11. James T. Farrell, *Studs Lonigan*, N.Y., Avon Books, A division of the Hearst Corporation, 1977.

12. John Steinbeck, *East of Eden*, N.Y., The Viking Press, 1952, p. 691.

13. Or like that of Brigitte Pian, the lady of François Mauriac's *Woman of the Pharisees*, N.Y., Farrar, Straus and Company, 1964).

14. Psalm 62:1–2.

15. It is encouraging that many theologians today are taking greater risks in demythologising, de-gnosticising, and de-platonising heaven and making it liveable again. For example, see: Sidney Callahan, *Exiled to Eden*, N.Y., Sheed and Ward, 1968, pp. 1–58. Also: Andrew Greeley, *Life for a Wanderer*, N.Y., Doubleday 1969, pp. 155–165.

16. John 6:67.

17. Matthew 25:1–13 and parallels.

18. Karl Rahner, 'The Celibacy of the Secular Priest Today', in *Servants of the Lord*, N.Y., Herder and Herder, 1968, Chapter 10, p. 152.

19. The Trial of Billy Jack. (This is not a direct quote, but a fairly accurate paraphrase – as well as I can remember it.)

20. Edward Malatesta, 'Jesus and Loneliness', in *The Way*, Vol. 16, October 1976, pp. 343–354.

21. *Idem.*

Chapter 9

1. This section, admittedly, is scant and inadequate. I will be able to do little more than point in a few directions, pinpoint a few necessary distinctions, highlight some existing bibliography, and propose a certain skeleton upon which such a spirituality might be built. To go further would necessitate another book. Hopefully those who see glaring inadequacies will be quick to offer fuller perspectives, for it is only important that we constantly find more satisfying answers. It is not so important where these come from.

2. There are already a number of good treatises written on precisely this point. Hence, I will limit myself to simply stating (rather than fully explaining) the main idea vis-à-vis the idea of risk. I would recommend reading:

– Andrew Greeley, *The Friendship Game*, N.Y., Sheed and Ward, 1971.

– John Powell, *The Secret of Staying in Love*, Niles, Illinois, Argus Communications, 1974.

– John Powell, *Why Am I Afraid to Love?* Niles, Illinois, Argus Communications, 1967.

– John Powell, *Why Am I Afraid to Tell You Who I Am?* Niles, Illinois, Argus Communications, 1969.

– Robert Lauder, *Loneliness Is for Loving*, Notre Dame, Ind., Ave Maria Press, 1978.

3. Vis-à-vis vulnerability: Here too there is already much good material available. See, for example:

– Henri Nouwen, *Intimacy, Pastoral Psychological Essays*, Notre Dame, Ind., Fides Publishers, 1970.

– Joseph Simons and Jeanne Reidy, *The Risk of Loving*, N.Y., Herder and Herder, 1968.

4. For this whole section on 'Free Space' I am indebted to Henri Nouwen. See: Henri Nouwen 'Reaching Out to Our Fellow Human Beings', in *Reaching Out*, N.Y., Doubleday, 1975, pp. 45–78.

5. Also see:

– Andrew Greeley, *The Friendship Game*, N.Y., Sheed and Ward, 1971.

– Andrew Greeley, *Sexual Intimacy*, Chicago, Thomas More Press, 1972.

6. I thank *Our Family* Magazine for allowing me to reprint material in this section which I had previously published in their December, 1976, issue. (See: 'Crucifixion: The Price of Togetherness', in *Our Family*, December 1976, © 1976 by Ronald Rolheiser omi.)

7. This whole section is hugely indebted to Henri Nouwen. See: Henri Nouwen, 'The First Movement: From Loneliness to Solitude', in *Reaching Out*, N.Y., Doubleday, 1975, pp. 13–44.

Also, see: Henri Nouwen, A Series of Articles on the Idea of Moving from Loneliness to Solitude, in the *National Catholic Reporter*, April 26–Sept. 5, 1974.

Nouwen has written excellently on this. I will do little more than briefly present some of his ideas on how to transform restless loneliness into solitude (though I will not always and everywhere be exactly faithful to his thinking). However, all the good ideas are his. I would heartily recommend that you read *Reaching Out*.

8. Henri Nouwen, *Reaching Out*, N.Y., Doubleday, 1975, p. 26. Also, see Nouwen's article, 'Isolate Self at Times', in *The National Catholic Reporter*, June 28, 1974.

9. *Idem.*

10. Again a huge debt is owed to Henri Nouwen, see: 'The Third Movement: From Illusion to Prayer', in *Reaching Out*, N.Y., Doubleday, 1975, pp. 79–117. Again, too, my approach will not always and everywhere be the same as his.

11. From the film *A Man for All Seasons* (a paraphrase – as well as I can remember it).

12. On this point see: Alvin Toffler, *Future Shock*, N.Y., Bantam Books, 1970, especially see the section 'Strategies for Survival', Chapters 17–20.

13. See William Hewett's article, 'Creative Loneliness', in *The Way*, Vol. 16, 1976, pp. 274–284, for further ideas on how to handle loneliness more creatively by writing.

A SELECTED BIBLIOGRAPHY ON LONELINESS

(A) Works which treat it as a problem within our Culture:

Becker, Ernst, 'The Spectrum of Loneliness,' in *Humanitas*, Vol. 10, 1974, pp. 237–247.

Bellah, Robert, *Habits of the Heart*, Berkeley, University of California Press, 1985.

Bier, William, (Ed.), *Alienation: Plight of Modern Man*, N.Y., Fordham University Press, 1972.

Bugbee, Henry, 'Loneliness, Solitude, and the Twofold Way in Which Concern Seems to Be Claimed,' in *Humanitas*, Vol. 10, 1974, pp. 313–329.

Dejanos, Sigmund, *Loneliness and Communication*, Toronto, Newman Press, 1971.

Delaczay, Etti, *Loneliness*, N.Y., Hawthorn Books, 1972. (A collection of 'wisdom' sayings on loneliness taken from various sources.)

Engelhardt, Tristam, 'Solitude and Sociality,' in *Humanitas*, Vol. 10, 1974, pp. 277–289.

Freud, Sigmund, *Civilization and Its Discontents*, London, The Hogarth Press, 1963.

Gordon, Suzanne, *Lonely in America, A Portrait of Americans, Young, Old, Married, Single, in Groups and Alone*, N.Y., A Touchstone Book, Simon and Schuster, 1976.

Gotesky, Rubin, 'Aloneness, Loneliness, Isolation, Solitude,' in *An Invitation to Phenomenology*, (James Edie, General Editor), Chicago, Quadrangle Books, 1965, pp. 211–240.

Gotz, Ignacio, 'Loneliness,' in *Humanitas*, Vol. 10, 1974, pp. 289–301.

Harper, Ralph, 'The Concentric Circle of Loneliness,' in *Humanitas*, Vol. 10, 1974, pp. 247–255.

Nostalgia: An Existential Explanation of Longing and Fulfillment in the Modern Age, Cleveland, Press of Western Reserve University, 1966.

The Seventh Solitude: Man's Isolation in Kierkegaard, Dostoevsky and Nietzsche, Baltimore, Johns Hopkins, 1965.

Jaspers, Karl, *Philosophy of Existence*, Philadelphia Press, 1971, p. 99.

Kaufmann, Bob, *Solitude Crowded with Loneliness*, N.Y., New Directions, 1965.

Kersten, Fred, 'Loneliness and Solitude,' in *Humanitas*, Vol. 10, 1974, pp. 301–313.

Krauss, Herbert and Beatrice, *Living with Anxiety and Depression*, Thomas More Press, 1974.

Lasch, Christopher, *The Culture of Narcissism*, N.Y., W. W. Norton, 1979.

Lotz, J. B., *The Problem of Loneliness*, N.Y., Alba House, 1967.

Maynard, Joyce, *Looking Back: A Chronicle of Growing Up Old in the Sixties*, N.Y., Doubleday, 1973, p. 160.

Moustakas, Clark, *Loneliness*, New Jersey, Prentice-Hall, 1961, p. 107.

Murchland, Bernard, (Ed.), *Age of Alienation: Fragmented Man*, N.Y., Random House, 1971.

Nabert, Jean, 'The Deepening of Solitude,' in *Elements for an Ethic*, Evanston, Northwestern University Press, 1969, pp. 30–38.

Ollman, Bertell, *Alienation: Marx's Conception of Man in Capitalist Society*, Cambridge University Press, 1971.

Riesman, David, *The Lonely Crowd*, New Haven, Yale University Press, 1970.

'The Lonely Crowd 20 Years After,' in *Encounter*, 1969, Oct., pp. 1–5.

Sadler, William, 'On the Verge of a Lonely Life,' in *Humanitas*, Vol. 10, 1974, pp. 255–277.

Siffre, Michel, 'Six Months Alone in a Cave,' in *National Geographic*, Vol. 147, No. 3, March 1975, pp. 426–435.

Slater, Philip, *The Pursuit of Loneliness: American Culture at the Breaking Point*, Boston, Beacon Press, 1970, p. 154.

Time, (Cover Story), 'The Porno Plague,' in *Time*, April, 1976.

Walker, Harold, *To Conquer Loneliness*, N.Y., Harper and Row, 1966.

Winter, Ruth, 'Why We Are Getting More Lonely,' in *San Francisco Chronicle*, Oct. 21, 1973, p. 4.

(B) LONELINESS – Theology and Spirituality:

Alive Now, (A bi-monthly publication by The Upper Room, 1908 Grand Avenue, Nashville, Tennessee 37203), A collection of excerpts and articles on 'Loneliness,' January–February issue, 1974.

Andrews, James F., *Creative Suffering: The Ripple of Hope*, Pilgrim Press, 1970.

Cailliet, Emile, 'Ultimate Spring of Solitude,' in *Christianity Today*, 1971, Vol. 15, (12).

Callahan, R. and Harlow, S., 'Loneliness and Religious Life,' in *Sisters Today*, Vol. 47, October, 1975, pp. 94–102.

Callahan, Sidney, *Exiled to Eden*, N.Y., Sheed and Ward, 1968, pp. 18–97.

Carroll, James, 'Hoping Sun, Sunny Hope,' in *National Catholic Reporter*, March 5, 1976.

Cummings, Charles, 'The Desert of Loneliness,' in *Spirituality and the Desert Experience*, New Jersey, Dimension Books, 1978, pp. 42–55.

Dalrymple, John, 'Alone with God,' in *The Way*, Vol. 16, 1976, pp. 284–290.

Day, Dorothy, *The Long Loneliness*, N.Y. Harper and Row, 1952, 1981.

Doherty, Catherine de Hueck, *Poustinia*, Notre Dame, Indiana, Ave Maria Press, 1975, pp. 23ff, and especially the last 2 chapters: 'My Own Poustinik Vocation,' and 'The Poustinia of the Heart.' (On the Loneliness of Jesus.)

Donnelly, Dorothy, 'And Loneliness Will Be No More,' in *Our Family*, Sept. 1976. pp. 2–5.

Drake-Brockman, David, *Birds of the Air*, N.Y., Paulist Press, 1982.

Duckworth, Ruth, 'Loneliness and Love,' in *The Way*, Vol. 16, 1976, pp. 266–274.

Dunne, John S., *The Reasons of the Heart. A Journey Into Solitude and Back Again Into the Human Circle*, N.Y., Macmillan Publishing Co., Inc., 1978.

The Homing Spirit, N.Y., Crossroad, 1987.

The House of Wisdom, San Francisco, Harper and Row, 1985.

Dyckman, Kathrine, and Carroll, Patrick, *Chaos or Creation?*, N.Y., Paulist Press, 1986.

Eberhard, Kenneth, *The Alienated Christian: A Theology of Alienation*, Philadelphia, Pilgrim Book, 1971.

Frank, Anne, *The Diary of Anne Frank*, N.Y., Doubleday, 1959.

Grant, Mary P., 'Fear and Loneliness,' in *The Way*, Vol. 16, 1976, pp. 254–266.

Greeley, Andrew, 'From Salvation of the Soul to Liberation of Person,' in *The New Agenda*, N.Y., Doubleday, 1973, pp. 168–201.

Sexual Intimacy, Thomas More Press, 1972.

The Friendship Game, Sheed and Ward, 1971.

Unsecular Man, N.Y., Schocken Books, 1972, p. 280.

Hageman, Louise Sr., *In the Midst of Winter*, Dimension Books, 1977.

Hammarskjold, Dag, *Markings*, London, Faber and Faber, 1964.

Hardon, John, *The Hungry Generation*, Maryland, Newman Press, 1967.

Heagle, John, *Life to the Full*, Chicago, Thomas More, 1976 (Especially Chapter 2.)

Hewett, William, 'Creative Loneliness,' in *The Way*, Vol. 16, 1976, pp. 274–284.

Israel, Martin, *Living Alone*, N.Y., Crossroad, 1983.

Kaiser, Albert, 'How to Cope with Loneliness,' in *Pastoral Life*, Jan. 1977, Vol. 26, pp. 33–36.

Kennedy, Eugene, *Living with Loneliness*, Chicago, Thomas More Press, 1973.

A Time for Love, N.Y., Doubleday, 1972.

Kerken, Libert Vander, *Loneliness and Love*, N.Y., Sheed and Ward, 1967.

Killinger, John, *All You Lonely People, All You Lovely People*, Waca, Texas, Ward Booking, 1973.

Lauder, Robert, *Loneliness Is for Loving*, Notre Dame, Ind., Ave Maria Press, 1978.

Lennon, T., 'Loneliness: A Christian Response,' in *St. Anthony Messenger*, Vol. 82, May 1975, pp. 1013.

Lentfoehr, T., 'Thomas Merton: The Dimensions of Solitude,' in *American Benedictine Review*, 1972, Vol. 23, pp. 337–352.

Lewis, C. S., *A Grief Observed*, N.Y., Macmillan, 1961.

Lynch, James, *The Broken Heart*, N.Y., Basic Books, 1977.

Madden, James P., Editor, *Loneliness: Issues of Emotional*

Living in an Age of Stress for Clergy and Religious. The Second Boston Psychotheological Symposium, Whitinsville, Massachusetts, Affirmation Books, 1977.

Malatesta, Edward, 'Jesus and Loneliness,' in *The Way*, Vol. 16, October 1976, pp. 343–353.

Maloney, Geo., *Inward Stillness*, Dimension Books, 1976, pp. 34ff.

Marasigan, V., 'Teilhard on Alienation,' in *The Teilhard Review*, July 1975, Vol. 10, pp. 46ff.

McDonnell, Thomas, 'Anatomy of Priestly Alienation,' in Pastoral Life, Feb. 1976, pp. 26–31.

Merton, Thomas, 'Christian Solitude,' in *Contemplation in a World of Action*, N.Y., Doubleday, 1973, pp. 252–264.

Moustakas, Clark, *Loneliness and Love*, N.J., Prentice-Hall Inc., 1972.

Neale, Robert, *Loneliness, Solitude and Companionship*, Philadelphia, Westminster Press, 1984.

Nouwen, Henri, *Intimacy*, Pastoral Psychological Essays, Notre Dame, Ind., Fides Publishers, 1970.

Out of Solitude, Notre Dame, Ind., Ave Maria Press, 1974.

Reaching Out, N.Y., Doubleday, 1975. (Much of the material covered in *Reaching Out* is contained as well in a series of articles in the *National Catholic Reporter*, April to December 1974. Also, Nouwen, himself, has made a tape of these ideas. See: 'The Lonely Search for God,' Thomas More Meditapes, c1974.)

The Genesee Diary, N.Y., Doubleday, 1976.

The Wounded Healer, N.Y., Doubleday, 1972.

Lifesigns: Intimacy, Fecundity and Ecstasy in Christian Perspective, N.Y., Doubleday 1986.

Oraison, Marc, *'The Fundamental Importance of Sexuality,'* in *The Human Mystery of Sexuality*, N.Y., Sheed and Ward, 1967, pp. 3–44.

Paige, H., 'The Gift of Loneliness,' in *Catholic Digest*, Vol. 39, July 1975, pp. 45–48.

Powell, John, *The Secret of Staying in Love*, Argus Communications, 1974.

Why Am I Afraid to Love? Argus Communications, 1967.

Why Am I Afraid to Tell You Who I Am? Argus Communications, 1969.

Quoist, Michel, *Prayers*, N.Y., Sheed and Ward, 1963, p. 179.

Riga, Peter, 'Death, Loneliness and Love,' in *Cross and Crown*, Dec. 1969, pp. 455–463.

Riley, J., 'How I Overcome Loneliness,' in *Ligourian*, Vol. 63, Sept. 1975, pp. 49–51.

Rilke, Rainer Maria, *Letters to a Young Poet*, W. W. Norton, 1954.

Selected Poems, Penguin Books, 1964.

Ripple, Paula, *Walking with Loneliness*, Notre Dame, Ave Maria Press, 1983.

Schoonenberg, Piet, 'Loneliness and Anxiety,' in *Man and Sin*, N.Y., Sheed and Ward, 1965, p. 205.

Scott, John M., 'The Last Word in Lonesome is Me,' Huntington, Indiana, Our Sunday Visitor, Inc., 1978.

Sell, Yvonne, 'Moving Towards God and Others,' in *Our Family*, Feb., 1978, pp. 4–8.

Simons, Joseph, and Reidy, Jeanne, *The Risk of Loving*, N.Y., Herder and Herder, 1968.

Tanner, Ira, *Loneliness: The Fear of Love*, N.Y., Harper and Row, 1973.

Wolffe, Richard, *The Meaning of Loneliness*, Wheaton, Ill., Key Publishers, 1970, p. 132.

Wurm, Sr. Mary Alice, 'Loneliness: Blessing or Threat?' in *Sisters Today*, Oct. 1971, Vol. 44, pp. 65–75.

Zorn, Robert L., and Ford, Edward E., *Why be Lonely?* Niles, Illinois, Argus Communications, 1975.

(C) On St. Augustine:

Augustine, in: *City of God*, X, 3.
                         XI, 13.
                         XIX, 11.
        De Genesi Contra Manichaeos I,20,31.
        De Trinitate, XIII, 5,8.

Bowmal, L., 'St. Augustine, The Restless Human Heart,' in *Cord*, Vol. 16, Sept., 1966, pp. 273–277.

Jones, W. T., *The Medieval Mind*, San Francisco, Harcourt, Brace and World, pp. 72–101.

Marcel, Gabriel, 'Uneasiness in St. Augustine,' in *Problematic Man*, N.Y., Herder, 1967, pp. 90–96.

Sheed, F. J., *Our Hearts Are Restless, The Prayer of St. Augustine*, N.Y., Seabury Press, 1976.

(D) On Thomas Aquinas:

Aquinas, Thomas, Sections of the *Summa Theologica*, and the
    Summa Contra Gentiles
  Summa Contra Gentiles: II,21
                           II,55
                           III, 25ff.
                           III, 69–70
  Summa Theologica I.q.1, a.7
                     I.q.12, a.
                     I.q.22, a.1
                     I.q.75, a.6
                     I.q.83, a.1–3
                     I.q.103, a.1
                     I/II, q.3,a.8
                     I/II,q.2,a.8
                     I/II,q.4,a.6
                     II/II,q.17, a.2

Donceel, Joseph, *Philosophical Anthropology*, N.Y., Sheed and
    Ward, c1967, p. 496.
Engelhardt, Paul, 'Thomism,' in *Sacramentum Mundi*, Vol. 6,
    Montreal, Palm Pub., c1970, pp. 249–255.

(E) On St. John of the Cross:

John of the Cross, *Ascent of Mount Carmel*, Book I, Chapters
    6–11. 'Living Flame of Love,' Commentary on Stanza 3, nos.
    18–25.

(F) On Karl Rahner:

America, October, 1970, (Oct. 31). A special issue on Rahner.
Donceel, Joseph, 'God and the Dynamism of the Mind: Karl
    Rahner,' in *Psyche and Spirit*, Edited by John J. Heaney,
    Toronto, Paulist Press, c1973, pp. 253–260.
Rahner, Karl, Articles in *Sacramentum Mundi* on: 'Beatific
    Vision,' 'Freedom,' 'Grace,' 'Man,' 'Order,' 'Parousia,'
    'Person,' 'Potentia Obedientalis.'
  'Experiment, Man,' in *Theology Digest*, Feb. 1968, pp. 57–69.
  Grace in Freedom, N.Y., Herder and Herder, c1969, p. 267.

Hearers of the Word, N.Y., Herder and Herder, c1969, p. 180.

Mission and Grace, N.Y., Sheed and Ward, 1963–66.

Nature and Grace: Dilemmas in the Modern Church, N.Y., Sheed and Ward, c1964, 149p.

Spirit in the World, N.Y., Herder and Herder, 1968, p. 408.

Theological Investigations, Volume II, Baltimore, Helicon Press, c1963, p. 363 (Cf. pp. 235–265) and Vol. IV, c1966, p. 421 (Cf. pp. 165–180).

Roper, Anita, *The Anonymous Christian*, With an Afterword – 'The Anonymous Christian According to Karl Rahner' – by Klaus Riesenhuber, N.Y., Sheed and Ward, p. 179.

Vorgrimler, Herbert, and Rahner, Karl, *Theological Dictionary*, Freiburg, Verlag, Herder, c1965, p. 493.

(G) Loneliness in Contemporary Literature and Poetry:

Bach, Richard, *Jonathan Livingston Seagull*, London, Pan Books, 1973.

Camus, Albert, *The Fall*, N.Y., Alfred Knopf, 1969, p. 147.

The Myth of Sisyphus and Other Essays, N.Y., Knopf, 1958.

The Stranger, N.Y., Knopf, 1946.

Eliot, T. S., *The Love Song of J. Alfred Prufrock*.

The Waste Land.

Farrell, James T., *Studs Lonigan*, Signet Book, 1958, p. 765.

Greene, Graham, *The End of the Affair*, London, Bodley Head, 1974.

Hesse, Herman, *Steppenwolf*, London, Penguin, 1969.

Laurence, Margaret, *The Stone Angel*, Toronto, McClelland and Stewart Limited, 1968.

Mauriac, François, *Woman of the Pharisees*, N.Y., The Noonday Press, Farrar, Straus and Company, 1964.

Moore, Brian, *The Lonely Passion of Judith Hearne*, Toronto, Little, Brown and Company, 1964.

Murdoch, Iris, *The Black Prince*, London, Chatto and Windus, 1984.

Nuns and Soldiers, London, Chatto and Windus, 1980.

The Sea, The Sea, London, Chatto and Windus, 1984.

Oates, Joyce Carol, *Them*, Greenwich, Conn., Fawcett Crest Book, 1970.

Rossner, Judith, *Looking for Mr. Goodbar*, N.Y., Pocket Books, Simon and Schuster, 1976.

Salinger, J. D., 'Uncle Wiggily in Connecticut,' in *Nine Short Stories*, Toronto, Bantam Books, Little, Brown and Company, 1964.

Susann, Jacqueline, *Valley of the Dolls*, N.Y., Bantam Books, 1967.

Tolstoy, Leo, *Anna Karenina*, London, Oxford University Press, 1980.

Updike, John, *Rabbit, Run*, London, André Deutsch, 1972.

Wolfe, Thomas, *The Hills Beyond*, N.Y., A Signet Classic, 1935.
Of Time and the River, A Signet Classic, 1966.
You Can't Go Home Again, A Signet Classic, 1966.
The Web and the Rock, A Signet Classic, 1966.

(Also on Thomas Wolfe see:)

Field, Leslie, *Thomas Wolfe: Three Decades of Criticism*, N.Y., New York University, 1968.

Nowell, Elizabeth, *Thomas Wolfe: A Biography*, N.Y., Doubleday, 1966.

Padovano, Anthony, 'Thomas Wolfe,' in *The Estranged God*, N.Y., Sheed and Ward, 1966, pp. 79–90.

Snyder, William, *Thomas Wolfe, Ulysses and Narcissus*, Athens, Ohio, Ohio University Press, 1971.

(H) Loneliness and Alienation in Art:

Corn, Wanda, *The Art of Andrew Wyeth*, N.Y., Graphic Society, Greenwich, Conn., 1973.

Wallace, Robert, *The World of Van Gogh*, Time Life Books, N.Y., 1969.

(I) Loneliness in Contemporary Music:

– ON 'ALIENATION-LONELINESS':
- – Eleanor Rigby – Beatles.
- – No Love at All – B. J. Thomas.
- – Sounds of Silence – Simon and Garfunkel.
- – At Seventeen – J. Ian.
- – Dying to Live – Edgar Winters.
- – Grover Hensan Feels Forgotten – Bill Cosby.
- – Poem on the Underground Wall – Simon and Garfunkel.
- – The Rose – Bette Midler.

- I Wanna Dance with Someone who Loves me – Whitney Houston.
- Cats in the Cradle – Harry Chapin.
- The Head and the Heart – Chris de Burgh.

– *ON 'RESTLESSNESS-LONELINESS'*:
- Richard Cory – Simon and Garfunkel.
- The Dangling Conversation – Simon and Garfunkel.
- I Am I Said – Neil Diamond.
- Torn Between Two Lovers – Mary MacGregor.
- Bird on a Wire – Jennifer Warnes.
- I Still Haven't Found What I'm Looking For – U2.

– *ON 'FANTASY-LONELINESS'*:
- Most Peculiar Man – Simon and Garfunkel.
- Save the Life of My Child – Simon and Garfunkel.
- The World of Make-Believe – The Moody Blues.
- Games People Play – Joe South.
- Dreams – Fleetwood Mac.
- Where Peaceful Waters Flow – Chris de Burgh.

– *ON 'ROOTLESSNESS-LONELINESS'*:
- Lost in a Lost World – The Moody Blues.
- The Candle of Love – The Moody Blues.
- Loneliness – America.
- So Far Away – Carole King.
- Touch Me in the Morning – Dianna Ross.
- Boy in the Bubble – Paul Simon.
- One Step Up – Bruce Springsteen.

– *ON 'BLUES-LONELINESS'*:
- Goodtime Charlie's Got the Blues – Danny O'Keefe.
- Jessie – Roberta Flack.
- Downtown – Petula Clark.
- Help Me Make It Through the Night – Samantha Smith.
- A Rainy Night in Georgia – Brooks Benton.
- Fatal Hesitation – Chris de Burgh.
- Spare Parts – Bruce Springsteen.